Sunny
the pil

A second later she shot up in her bed. Only, it wasn't *her* bed. Or even night. Sun was shining in the bedroom window.

"What's wrong?" Nick tugged her arm till she turned.

Just looking at him took her breath away. All dark and tawny, sprawled in white cotton sheets. There should be a law against looking so sinful and downright inviting. Her body was already gearing up to accept that invitation, too.

"I have to leave," she said nervously.

"There you go, *having* to do something again." He shifted and the sheet moved dangerously low on his hips. "What's really wrong?"

Her mouth went dry. "I—I spent the night."

"And this is a problem—why?"

"Because I don't spend the night."

Nick propped himself up on his pillow. "Oh?"

"Spending the night leads to speculation," she said. "On the part of the person you spend it with."

Nick grinned and reached for her. "And what's wrong with that...?"

Donna Kauffman is the award-winning, nationally bestselling author of eighteen contemporary romance novels. She worked as a bookkeeper, dog groomer, people groomer, art instructor and competitive bodybuilder before turning to storytelling. She began writing while expecting her first child, put the manuscript aside, then finished it during a second pregnancy. That book became her first published novel. She's since written many more, calling on both imagination and background in order to create compelling, innovative stories.

Walk on the Wild Side is Donna's debut book for Temptation. It's a fun, sexy story about a wealthy heroine who longs to take a walk in the real world, albeit temporarily. The passion and love she finds with Nick is worth the trip alone. Look for more books from this talented writer who loves to hear from her fans. Check out her Web site at www.donnakauffman.com. Enjoy!

WALK ON THE WILD SIDE
Donna Kauffman

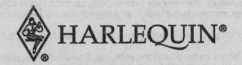

HARLEQUIN®

TORONTO • NEW YORK • LONDON
AMSTERDAM • PARIS • SYDNEY • HAMBURG
STOCKHOLM • ATHENS • TOKYO • MILAN • MADRID
PRAGUE • WARSAW • BUDAPEST • AUCKLAND

This book is dedicated to my "sister," Jill Shalvis.

Families aren't always the ones you're born into.

Thanks for taking that first step
and making us a family.

ISBN 0-373-25928-X

WALK ON THE WILD SIDE

Copyright © 2001 by Donna Jean.

_____Prologue_____

"YOUR PLACE is with the family, heading the company," said Edwin Chandler, rebuking his granddaughter. "There will be no further nonsense about this...this sabbatical you wish to take."

Susan Haddon Chandler kept her gaze focused outside the tinted limousine window. Otherwise the sight of her grandfather's sharply disapproving expression might just tempt her to strangle him. Which would be exceedingly foolish. Then she'd have to take over the business immediately.

"Susan, are you paying attention? I didn't raise you to be rude."

No, she thought wearily, she was raised to be cold, unfeeling, totally focused on business and the bottom line—exactly like her grandparents were. To hell with love, life and anything resembling a good time.

And she hated being called Susan. Her grandparents were the only people in her life who didn't call her Sunny. That nickname was the one nice thing her father had given her before he and her mother had died in a yacht racing accident right before her fifth birthday.

Almost from that day forward, she'd known *this* day was coming. She'd always believed that she'd somehow find a way to accept the inevitable when the time came. Every other person in her graduating class had clutched their diploma like the ticket to freedom it represented.

She hadn't, though. Her degrees represented a one-way ticket to life imprisonment inside the block of cold granite and steel that housed Chandler Enterprises. She would be expected to remain in her suite of rooms in Haddon Hall, the ancestral home of her maternal great-great-grandmother, where her grandparents could continue to monitor her every breath.

How did she say, "Thanks, but no thanks," to the people who had given her everything?

She hazarded a glance at her grandfather and felt her spirits sink even lower. There were no words that would penetrate that stubborn piece of stone he called a heart.

"Grandfather, I'm not trying to upset you," she began.

"Well, you're going about it very well indeed. I'm not getting any younger. It's time to curb this foolishness."

Her grandfather was seventy-eight. But he still put in a full workweek and then some. She knew he would continue to do so until he dropped dead, preferably while heading an international board meeting, closing yet another multimillion-dollar deal. She was fairly certain there was a clause somewhere on her birth certificate that said she was expected to do the same.

"I'm finally done with grad school. I don't think it's foolish to want to spend some time on my own," she reasoned. "You know how much I appreciate all you and Grandmother have done for me. And I'm not turning my back on Chandler Enterprises." The critical look he gave her only firmed her resolve. She was no shrinking violet. Edwin had seen to that early on. Well, now he would have to deal with the mini-me he'd created.

"I fully intend to take my place in the company," she told him. "But you have no intentions of stepping down any time soon. Six months will not alter our plans significantly. I'm only twenty-five. I have the rest of my life to devote to Chandler Enterprises. I'm only asking for six months."

"You had plenty of time on your own in school."

No, I didn't, she thought stubbornly. Her grandparents had chosen the sorority she pledged, made certain she only roomed with girls from suitable families and checked up on her constantly. That was when they weren't demanding she fly home every other week for some social function or other.

She tried again. "It's not like I'm planning to cut myself off from you and Grandmother. I'll even stay here in Chicago. I just need enough time to learn a bit more about who I am—"

"The one thing you can certainly never doubt is who you are, Susan. And six months might as well be an eternity. You know about the upcoming merger. If you are to ever head this company, now is the time to step in, to be in on the new direction we are taking from the day the papers are signed. I expect you to participate in the meetings we have scheduled and more important, I expect you to help Frances and me host the variety of social events that will go hand in hand with this monumental event in the history of Chandler Enterprises. You know as well as I do that more business takes place at those functions than in the boardroom. I expect you to shine, to take your rightful place beside me and move into the inner circle."

Her grandfather's words turned into a toneless hum inside her head as her panic began to swell. The more he talked about his expectations, the faster the panic grew. She had to get out. *Now.*

The limo was taking her from their luncheon meeting, where Edwin had laid out her future in no uncertain terms, to the Chandler Enterprises empire. She had this overwhelming fear that once she arrived inside that building, she'd be locked into her future forever. She had the degree, she had the training, both socially and educationally. But she didn't have the heart for it.

She wasn't sure she ever would.

She looked out of the window, despair close to consuming her. And that is when she saw the sign.

Kitchen Help Wanted. Full Time.

"Driver, stop the car!"

"Susan! What in the devil—"

"Stop the car right now, please."

"Carl, don't listen to—"

But Carl had pulled the sleek automobile to the curb, and Susan was leaping out. She paused long enough to lean in and beseech her grandfather one last time. "I know you don't understand this and I'm truly sorry for that. It's only six months. Then I'll be the best little Chandler this family has ever bred. I promise."

Her grandfather's face was so red she suddenly feared she'd pushed him over the edge into a stroke or a heart attack. She was halfway back in the car when he erupted.

"What I understand is that you're apparently more immature than Frances and I had assumed. You seriously disappoint me, Susan. This little escapade of yours will cost you far more than it will cost me. You'll soon find out you don't know the first thing about living in the so-called real world. You want six months? You won't last six days."

That was his final mistake. It was like waving a red flag. Anyone who had ever done business with a Chandler learned very early on to never, ever challenge them. Not if they expected to win. Chandlers always won. Of course, now it was Chandler versus Chandler. Sunny hated that it had come to this, but she'd be damned if she'd back down.

"Then I'll learn. I'm bright. I have the degrees to prove it." And with that she closed the door. The door to her past, her carefully planned future and everything she'd ever known.

She turned away and strode to the small Italian restaurant she'd spied from the street. She opened the door and removed the sign from the window. She didn't know the first thing about what this job involved. But she was a Chandler, and when she left this restaurant today, she'd be leaving it as their newest employee.

She saw the limo pull away from the curb in the reflection of the window. "Goodbye, Chandler Enterprises," she whispered. She looked at the sign over the door. "Hello, D'Angelos."

1

THE RESTAURANT DOOR closed behind her. Sunny was immediately assaulted with hot, steamy air. The slow-moving ceiling fans swirled thick scents of sausage and spices and other things she couldn't name but were making her mouth water and her stomach grumble.

The decor reflected the restaurant's homey, inviting size. Traditional red-checked tablecloths, slender candles and soft white linen napkins were arranged on every table. There were large round tables dominating the center of the room, where she could picture families boisterously talking as they enjoyed their meals. The walls were dotted with smaller, more intimate tables tucked into alcoves. Those private tables were ideal for a romantic dinner. Vivid Italian landscapes covered the warm yellow walls, vined plants were tucked into ceiling alcoves and draped across the lattice separating the smaller tables.

Everything about D'Angelos was like a warm, welcoming hug.

Everything Chandler Hall had never been.

She was instantly entranced. Fate had brought her

here, she was certain of it. If she had any lingering doubts about what she'd just done, she swallowed them.

An older, apron-clad woman came out from the back. She was quite short, and just as stout, with her salt-and-pepper hair caught in a surprisingly lush bun on top of her head. She smiled broadly on seeing Sunny standing there, sign in hand, and Sunny smiled back. It went a long way toward easing the sudden wobbly feeling she had in her knees.

"You're here for the position?" the woman said, her accent a mix of Italian and pure Chicago.

Sunny stepped forward and held out her hand. "I'm Sunny Chandler, and yes, I'm here for the job."

The woman took her hand and gave it a shake that almost had Sunny wincing. She had to be close to Edwin's age, judging from the lines on her face and the mottled skin on the back of her hand. Sunny liked her instantly.

"You have qualifications? References?"

Sunny faltered, but only briefly. Shoulders straight, she held the woman's gaze and spoke earnestly. "No references, but I trained at the Jean Marc Academy for two years." And hated every minute. "I graduated with honors." Although that had mostly been to annoy the insufferable Jean Marc.

"And when did you earn this certificate?"

Sunny's face heated, but her posture remained proud. "I was fourteen, ma'am."

The old woman laughed. Heartily.

"Is there a problem? I assure you I'm a quick study and a hard worker."

"You need this job, eh?" She waved her silent when Sunny started to speak. "You are here, so you are willing. What I wish to know is *why* you are here." She motioned to the closest table. "Sit. You will tell me what brought you to D'Angelos today. Then I will decide on your future employment. That will be your résumé."

Sunny sat. The other woman sat, as well, and held out her hand. "I am Benedictine D'Angelo. Everyone calls me Mama Bennie."

"Pleased to meet you, Mrs. D'Angelo."

The woman tsked and shook her head. "Are you not an everyone?"

"I'd be honored to be an everyone. I'd love to call you Mama Bennie if you'd let me. You can call me Sunny."

The woman nodded, her smile a gleaming one. "You have a smile as bright as your name. And I like your style."

Sunny grinned. "The feeling is mutual."

Bennie looked her over. "You are wearing clothing worth more than you will likely earn here in months. You speak in cultured tones that tell me you have diplomas from schools other than Jean Marc's." She leaned forward, all but pinning Sunny to her seat with her dark eyes. "So, why don't you get to the meat of it?"

Sunny smiled, thankful for Bennie's straightforward style. She told her the whole story.

Mama Bennie was frowning. "Seems your grandfather feels respect goes only one way. D'Angelos doesn't operate like that. We're a very close family, but love means you allow those you love to find their own happiness. Fortunately, many D'Angelos have found their happiness here. We're a third-generation restaurant. Almost all run by D'Angelos."

"Why the sign then?"

"My youngest grandson, Joey, is off to graduate school this fall. He's a computer programmer. Designs those crazy computer games all the kids are playing." She shrugged as if to say it was beyond her, but her smile returned quickly. "He's smart, our Joey. Full scholarship. But he got a summer job on campus with one of his professors, so he's leaving a bit earlier than we'd expected. I don't have anyone else in place at the moment, so the sign went up."

Sunny felt like providence was shining down on her. "So, the job is a temporary one? Until you find a family member?"

"It doesn't have to be." She eyed Sunny meaningfully.

It was a perfect setup. They could fill each other's needs until it didn't suit them any longer. When the time came, she'd go back to Chandlers, and another

D'Angelo would fill her position. "I think I came to the right place."

"I think so, too. But I must be honest with you, Sunny. I am old-fashioned enough to wish you were a good Italian girl. But I'm also old enough to enjoy upsetting the applecart from time to time." She winked, then got down to business. "I'm going to have to insist on a one-month probationary period. Just to make sure you can live up to that fancy gourmet diploma you earned."

Sunny blushed, feeling foolish for her earlier airs. "I won't let you down, Mama Bennie."

"I believe you'll try, and that's the best I can hope for. Now, there is one more thing before we fill out the paperwork. A minor bit of business, really."

She had the job! Sunny was so relieved, nothing else mattered at this point. "I'm sure whatever it is, I—"

"Not whatever, *whoever*." Mama Bennie pushed her chair back and stood, "Follow me."

Sunny followed the older woman toward the back of the restaurant. They passed the double doors leading to the kitchen. There was a sudden burst of violent Italian, followed by the clash and clang of several pots and pans, followed once more with voices raised in a heated argument.

She paused a moment before Mama Bennie took her arm and continued down the hallway.

"Come, come. Don't mind Carlo. He's a hothead, but a pussycat on the inside. Really."

Sunny wasn't so sure about that. Another crash made her wince and look over her shoulder in the direction of the swinging doors. Just what had she gotten herself into?

She barely had time to finish that thought when Mama Bennie knocked once on a large wooden door then pushed it open without waiting for a response.

"Niccolo, I have our new kitchen help here. I wish her to begin immediately. I just need the papers." Before Sunny could gather her wits, Mama Bennie thrust her in front of her ample bosom.

The man she faced could only be called imposing. And that was only partly due to his height. They were in a stockroom, and he'd been surveying the contents stacked on the crowded shelving units, a clipboard in his hand. Now he was staring at her. Unlike Mama Bennie, he didn't welcome her with a warm smile. Not even close.

He wore black pants and a white button-down shirt with the collar undone. The sleeves were rolled up haphazardly over healthy-size forearms. She could see his white undershirt through the cotton. It was the old-fashioned tank style. She didn't think they made those anymore. Something about the way it defined his chest and shoulders caught her attention. She jerked her gaze to his face, only to feel another little shock of awareness.

His eyes were a bottomless brown with thick lashes that should have been illegal on a man. And his hair all but begged a woman to sink her fingers into it. It was thick and dark and a bit wild, as if he'd just recently left the steam-soaked kitchen. She could easily imagine him all hot and passionate, shouting in Italian. That thought had her looking at his mouth. Big mistake. It was full, generous, even compressed in a hard line as it was now. Suddenly all thoughts of steamy rooms and heated emotions had her normally well-ordered mind racing in directions it never had before. It was like he'd found her hormonal On button and flipped it. Hard.

Then he shifted his focus away from her, and the switch flipped abruptly to Off.

"We're not hiring anyone who looks like her to work in my kitchen."

Mama Bennic snapped out something in Italian, which Sunny only partly caught, but the smoldering man before her curbed his tongue. His expression, however, remained heated. She didn't think it was about hormones, though. Just as well. Sexist jerk. Probably the head chef or something. They were all temperamental. She'd figured that out at fourteen. So what if he was the embodiment of every red-blooded woman's Italian stud fantasies?

Just because she looked like the stereotypical blue-eyed blond WASP she was didn't mean she couldn't make her way here in this swarthy, testosterone-laden little world of his. She'd won over Jean Marc, who could give lessons to this guy in testosterone spewing. She'd even won over Mama Bennie. She'd win over this guy, too. After all, winning was what Chandlers did best. She wondered briefly how her grandfather would react when she told him she owed her new job to his formative training.

So there she was, all primed and ready to do battle for blond, blue-eyed princesses everywhere, when Mama Bennie promptly took the wind out of her sails.

"Sunny Chandler, this narrow-minded young man is my grandson Nick D'Angelo. Despite his more obvious flaws, he's good at what he does. He's the third-generation D'Angelo to run this whole operation." She beamed at them both. "He's your new boss."

2

"WOULD YOU MIND waiting out in the hall?" Nick didn't give the young woman a chance to say no. He took her arm and steered her toward the door.

He supposed he shouldn't have been surprised when she yanked her arm free, resisting his assistance. When Mama Bennie stuck her nose in the family business, trouble always seemed to follow.

"Thank you," she said in that oh-so-polite tone. "But I really think, if we're going to be working together, that we reach an understanding right off."

Nick scowled at Bennie's approving smile.

"I'll leave you two to work out the details," she said, slipping out before Nick could stop her. She was seventy-six and shaped like a ravioli, but she could move with amazing speed when necessary.

Nick forced his fingers to relax on the clipboard and turned once again to face his latest entrant in the Marry Off Niccolo Sweepstakes. Mama Bennie must be getting desperate. This one wasn't even Italian.

"I'm sorry, but you've wasted your time."

Ms. Chandler planted her hands on her slender

hips. "Do you, or do you not, wish to hire kitchen help?"

Nick sighed heavily. "I do. But I also do the hiring. And the firing," he added with a pointed look. "Mama Bennie means well, but I'll be frank with you. She only gave you the job because you're young and beautiful."

"Really," she said, polished smile intact. "I promise you, I didn't come in here expecting to get this job based on my good looks."

Nick folded his arms, clipboard and all. "Oh? And just what qualifications do you have? We only seat seventy-five, but we offer a full menu. I need someone with experience working a kitchen under those kinds of demands. Do you have experience with Italian cuisine? Southern? Northern?"

His barrage of questions had been designed to make her understand in no uncertain terms exactly why he wasn't hiring her.

She looked deflated and defeated. He tried to ignore the twinge of guilt he felt. So what if he was a soft touch for the occasional sob story? He still wasn't hiring her. He supposed he could let her down easy, though. He blew out a long sigh and tried on his kinder, gentler voice.

"Listen, I have two weddings and a communion to cater in the next ten days, along with an annual street festival to prepare for. If I don't get this order called in by three this afternoon, I'm going to have an angry mother of the bride on my hands, as well. I simply don't have time to train anyone right now. I'm sure you'll find something somewhere else. There are plenty of people hiring these days."

He thought he'd done pretty well under the circumstances, but one look at her told him she didn't appreciate his kind and gentle routine. So much for the easy letdown.

Somewhere between the angry mother-in-law and the no-time-to-train-you part, her chin had come up, showing off the rope of matched pearls adorning her neck, and her slender shoulders had squared beneath the designer blouse she wore. He should have gone with his original instinct and hauled her out bodily. But she was talking, and he found himself listening. Her teeth were white and straight, her lips exactly the right width and curved just so. He should have been turned completely off, as perfection rarely called to him.

He was drawn more toward the slightly offbeat, the woman with that one crooked tooth or a smile that was a bit too wide, eyebrows a bit uneven. A woman with a bit of the Windy City or the old country in her voice. With hips a bit too wide, breasts on the luxurious side and hair…lots of hair. Thick, wavy hair made to sink his fingers into. That was the kind of woman who got his attention without even trying.

Not this cool, blond, slim drink of imported water with a twist of lemon, please.

And yet, he was all but hanging on her every word.

"Actually," she said, with just the right amount of defensive posturing, "my experience is more Continental. French cuisine. Mama Bennie agreed to give me a one-month probationary period. Surely you can give me that much of a trial. If I don't pull my weight, you can give me the ax. Fair?"

No, he thought, it wasn't fair. He didn't have time for this. And he certainly didn't have time to figure out what it was about her that got his complete attention. He had zero time for that. Less than zero. So why in the world he opened his mouth and said, "One month. I want that in writing, so when I fire you, you won't bring in some fancy suit and sue me," he had no idea.

She smiled with satisfaction, which irked him all the more. She might not have wanted to trade on her good looks, but Nick could think of no reason other than his unreliable hormones for what he'd just gone and done. She stuck out her hand, and he actually had to think about the consequences of touching her.

He almost laughed. Damn if she hadn't reduced him to the level of a gawky teenager, sweating out his first kiss. Only he'd never been gawky, as a teenager or any other time. He'd always been a natural with women. At twenty-eight, he could certainly handle this one.

He took her hand and pumped it once, then let it drop. Warm. He hadn't expected that. He'd expected cool, finely boned, impersonal. He'd gotten two out of three right, but that one wrong had been critical.

Warm, huh? He found himself glancing into those blue eyes. Ice princess? Or blond temptress?

He shook the thoughts from his head. She was an employee now, he reminded himself. He did have some boundaries, and that was one of them. No dating the boss.

"So, where do I begin?" She asked expectantly.

He cleared his throat. "There is some paperwork to fill out. Don't you want to discuss salary?"

It was her turn to look momentarily nonplussed. "Oh, uh, right. I suppose so, yes. I guess I assumed I'd just start out at the standard rate for new employees." She forced a smile to cover what they both knew was a lame attempt to sound like an everyday new hire.

Which he knew she was not.

"So, you don't care about the money? Why *do* you need this job? Really."

"I always care about the money," she corrected. "It's bred into the Chandler DNA."

"Chandler?" He recalled Bennie's introduction. Sunny Chandler. Understanding dawned. "As in Chandler Enterprises?"

"I'm related, yes. You're not going to fire me now, are you?"

"Why should I give this job to you instead of someone who really does need employment?"

"There are plenty of jobs out there. No one will go

jobless because you hired me. So why not? I'm available."

"And why is that?"

Her smile slipped a little, but she caught it on her chin, which lifted just enough to save it. "I'd rather not go into the details."

"You told Bennie."

She opened her mouth, as if to deny it, but shut it and nodded. "You can ask her if you want. I didn't swear her to secrecy."

Nick swore under his breath. If Bennie considered Sunny one of her worthy causes, he'd have a hell of a time getting rid of her. "And she thinks I'm a soft touch," he muttered.

"I hardly think of you as a soft touch."

"I hired you, didn't I?" he retorted, briefly enjoying a look of surprise, then dismay, on her face. He'd bet his last dollar she was not remotely used to being a pity case.

"I agreed to a short trial period after which I can be fired, no questions asked. Isn't that enough?"

He was dying to know what was really going on here, and damned if he'd go running to Bennie to find out. One way or the other, he'd get her to spill the real reason she'd invaded his life. Right before he fired her and got back to business. "Rather argumentative for someone who wants a job here so badly."

He could see her grit her teeth, but she remained outwardly calm. "I'm simply being logical."

"Logically I should hire someone with experience."

"In one month, if I don't fit the bill, you can."

"You're a tough negotiator. Is that also in the Chandler DNA?"

"You bet." She rubbed her palms gently on her pants. Nervous? He wouldn't have thought it of her. "Where are the papers for me to sign?"

"Anxious?"

She grinned at him. "I only have one month to impress the boss. I don't plan on wasting any time."

Despite the chaos this escapade of hers was likely to create, his responding smile was remarkably natural and relaxed. He'd just realized she hadn't met her co-workers yet. This might be the shortest trial period on record.

"I'll get to them after I finish my order. Bennie will take you to the kitchen and introduce you to the head chef. For all intents and purposes, he will be your immediate boss." His smile spread at her look of alarm. She'd begged for this job. He wasn't going to apologize for the working conditions. "Just consider me the CEO."

"The head chef...that wouldn't be—"

"Carlo." He nodded. "I see you've already met."

"Not exactly."

Nick shouldn't be enjoying this so much. Really. But she was so damned cool and competent. Competent—at least in her world—he had no doubt. He remembered her warm palm brushing his. The cool part was still in question.

He reminded himself that if she walked out today, he wouldn't go in search of the answer. She was from another world, another stratosphere, really. It wasn't that he thought her better than himself, but there were some cultural bridges too exhausting to span just for the fun of it. He'd give this one a pass.

"I'm not sure where Bennie is at the moment," he said. "So why don't I introduce you to Carlo myself."

"You just want to watch the fireworks," she muttered.

"What was that?"

She smiled brightly at him, her eyes telling him she knew he'd heard her. "I said I can't wait to see how all this works." She waved a hand. "Lead on."

He opened the door and waved a hand of his own. "Ladies first."

"Don't you mean lions?" she asked dryly.

Nick laughed at that. "The lions generally won against the gladiators."

"Not the ones armed with sharp blades, they didn't."

Damn if he didn't admire her sense of humor. He didn't give her a chance in hell of making it to the end of the day, but something had driven her to this. That softened him a bit. After all, it was only one day. "Carlo isn't as bad as all that. His bark is worse than his bite."

"But he *does* bite," she countered. "I thought so." Then, with a toss of her blond lioness mane, she walked into the hall. "As long as he realizes I bite back, we'll get along just fine."

Behind her, Nick's smile faded a bit. Maybe that's exactly what he should be afraid of.

3

ELEVEN HOURS LATER, Sunny collapsed into a chair outside the kitchen doors. She rested her elbows onto a table and dropped her head into her hands. "I'd rather oversee a hostile takeover than do this again." A glass of ice water appeared in front of her. She swallowed most of it in one gulp, eyes closed in abject appreciation. She pulled off her hairnet and pushed at the straggling strands stuck to her forehead, then gazed at her savior, relieved to find it was Mama Bennie.

Nick had hovered all night. Inevitably, she'd glance up from whatever merciless task Carlo had dictated she perform, only to find him watching her. Probably hoping she'd do something really stupid so he could fire her on the spot. But something about the way he watched her made her insides twitch. Sort of like when the skin between her shoulder blades itched and she couldn't reach the spot to scratch it.

"You did well in there tonight," the older woman said with a proud nod.

Sunny winced as she toed out of her borrowed

sneakers. "I survived," she corrected. "I think. I'm still not certain how I managed it."

Mama Bennie took a seat across from her and folded her arms on the table. "You managed fine."

Sunny didn't want to think about the past eleven hours. Since the moment Nick had introduced her to Carlo and his staff, she felt she'd been treading water in a whirlpool. Barely.

Mama Bennie patted her hand. "You'll do even better tomorrow."

Sunny took pride in the fact that she didn't fling herself on the floor screaming right then and there. Another night like this one and she'd crawl home over glass to her grandparents.

Nick appeared from the back and drew out the chair at the table next to theirs. He straddled it and smiled at Sunny. The smugness in that smile made her grit her teeth, but she knew she looked like over-boiled pasta at the moment, so there was little she could say in her own defense. In his place, she'd probably be a bit smug, too.

"Good thing we were quiet tonight," Nick said smoothly. "Gave you a chance to break into the routine slowly."

Slowly! That was slowly? She downed the rest of her water.

"She did a good job, Niccolo," Mama Bennie said. "She's a sharp one. She'll learn quickly, you'll see."

At a shout from the back, Mama Bennie excused herself and left them alone. Together.

Sunny felt that itch again as he stared at her. She figured her night was about to get worse. How that was possible was beyond her.

The argument with her grandfather seemed like two lifetimes ago. She'd started working this afternoon bent on proving her grandfather wrong. But after Nick's fifth or sixth visit to the kitchen, she realized she was also doing it to prove Nick wrong. His opinion of her ability to function outside her rarefied world wasn't much higher than Edwin's.

Well, her stubbornness had gotten her through one endless shift. But at that moment, she was pretty sure she'd rather eat crow in front of Nick, Edwin and the entire Chandler Enterprises board of directors than attempt to survive another shift. She opened her mouth, prepared to give him the words he wanted to hear and deal with his humiliating I told you so, but he spoke first.

"I talked to Carlo before he left. He isn't happy with me for hiring you at the moment."

She looked at him. "I did everything he asked me to do."

"His main concern is speed. When this place is full, we're going to need someone who can do what is expected, do it well and not take all night to get it done."

A slow burn started, making her stomach jumpy

and her nerves even more ragged. "I wasn't going slow to make anyone angry. I was doing my job to the best of my abilities."

"Well, Carlo says he appreciates that you are a perfectionist. He understands pride in a job well done. However, washing vegetables isn't an art form. If you want to continue here, your speed will have to improve."

Sunny opened her mouth to tell him what he could do with his vegetables, clean or otherwise, but to her surprise, what came out was, "What time do I start tomorrow?"

She took a measure of pleasure in the obvious surprise that lit his dark eyes. Good, she thought. "I didn't graduate in the top ten in my class by giving up when the going got tough," she said, enjoying his sudden consternation. It was likely the only reward she would get for her hard hours of labor, so she decided to enjoy it as fully as possible. "If you think that Carlo's bullying tactics will make me run home to Granddaddy, think again."

Dear God, what was she saying? She was going to do this? Again?

She looked at the frown pulling at the corners of his oh-so-incredible mouth. The same mouth that had been smiling smugly at her moments before. Yeah, she thought, that was exactly what she was doing. She made a mental note to get up in time to find some comfortable shoes, extra padded bandages for the blisters on her heels and something to securely pin up her hair.

"Your shift starts at four," he said tightly.

"I'll be here at three." At his raised eyebrow, she added, "I will use my own time to familiarize myself better with what is expected of me."

"I have no time to train you. You'll have to ask—"

"I've already talked to Romano. He's going to come in early and help me."

"I'll just bet he is," Nick muttered darkly. He shoved his chair forward and stood. "I still have paperwork to do. Use the rear employee door to come and go from now on."

She resisted the impulse to salute him. "Yes, sir." He turned away, but stopped when she added, "Thank you."

He turned to face her. "For what?"

"Giving me a chance," she said sincerely. "I know you don't understand why this is important to me, but I promise I won't make you any sorrier than you already are for letting Mama Bennie talk you into this."

His stiff posture relaxed a fraction. "It won't be the last time I do something foolish because she wants me to."

"I'll make Mama Bennie proud." *And you*, she thought, then rapidly backtracked. What he thought of her wasn't important. "You're lucky to have a grandmother who loves you so much."

He looked at her. "You say that as if you don't have the same. Your grandmother would be..." He paused, then said, "Frances. Frances Chandler." He laughed. "Don't look so startled. I may not have the fancy degree, but I do read the papers."

Sunny wished she hadn't guided the conversation in such a personal direction. She smoothed another loose strand of hair and sat up straighter. Her lower back screamed in protest. She ignored it. Chandlers never let the opposition see their weaknesses. "My grandparents love me very much. It's just...well, they show it in a different way than yours."

She stood as a discouragement to further conversation, then swallowed a groan when the arches of her feet relaxed against the wood floor. No way was she going to be able to get into the heels she'd been wearing. Maybe ever. She'd have to fake it across the back alley to her—

Car. She had no car. And at one in the morning, getting a cab in this neighborhood wasn't going to be easy. "Can I use the office phone? It's a local call."

He didn't say anything for a moment, then relented, sweeping his arm in front of him. "After you."

It took all her waning willpower to walk down the hall in front of him without limping. "I'll get my things from my locker."

"I'd rather you make your call first, so I can get back to work."

She nodded, too busy trying to figure out where

she was going to sleep tonight to argue. One thing she couldn't argue was that, for all Nick demanded a lot of his employees, he appeared to work just as hard, if not harder.

He opened the door and ushered her in, flipping on the light as he passed her. She looked around Nick's cramped office. An antique oak desk piled high with papers, books and file folders dominated the room. The walls were covered with pictures of Nick with family and friends as well as with some local and national celebrities. There were also a couple pictures of an older man who could have been his father or his grandfather.

"Salvatore D'Angelo," he said, apparently catching her interest. "My grandfather. Bennie's husband. He came over from Italy when he was only twenty. Started this restaurant before he turned thirty. He passed away five years ago."

"I'm sorry," she said. "I bet he and Bennie made a great team."

Nick came to stand just behind her. He was silent, which was good, since somehow there was less air in the room than moments before.

She was about to move away when he spoke. "Papa Sal understood people. He knew everyone in this neighborhood by name. He knew when someone was going through a tough time, and he knew before anyone else when a wedding was going to take place. Everyone sought him out for advice. He never turned anyone away. He treated the well known like they were from the neighborhood and the neighborhood people like they were stars. We all miss him terribly."

His softly spoken words made her eyes burn. "Being that well-loved is a wonderful reward for a life well lived," she said. "I'm sure he'll live a long time in the hearts of those who knew him."

"He'd have probably liked you." She stilled when Nick's hand landed on her shoulder. Just as quickly, he dropped it. "He was a good one for bucking traditions. He liked to make people reexamine their preconceptions."

Feeling oddly exposed, she slid from between him and the wall and faced him. "It must be hard," she said, "feeling like you have to fill his shoes." She realized then that they had something in common. The burden of following in their family's footsteps.

"It's a challenge, but one I won't ever walk away from. My parents died when we were kids. Sal and Bennie raised all of us, but as the oldest, I knew I would run D'Angelo's. Sal saw to it that I was as ready as I could be before he left us." He eyed her deliberately, and she figured Mama Bennie had told him her story.

Well, fine. She was too tired to argue. Let him think what he wanted about her. He didn't look away, and neither, she discovered, could she. Despite her fatigue and the distraction of her other problems, she felt energy fairly radiating from him. It made her thinly stretched nerves fray a little bit more. There was no denying the man had sex appeal in spades. And then there was his voice. When he talked passionately, as he had moments ago, all sorts of inappropriate things she'd like to hear him say in that same intimate voice sprung to her mind. On top of everything else, sexual tension had no place in her life.

She broke eye contact and turned toward the desk, intent on finding the phone. She caught sight of herself in a small antique mirror tucked in among the pictures and almost laughed. She looked like a raccoon that had run a marathon. And come in last. Mascara ringed her eyes, her hair was damp and stringy, and her skin was pasty. Except for two pink spots on her cheek and a red nose. From the steam, most likely.

Oh, yeah, sexual tension was going to be a big problem. *Not.* And he thought she got by on her good looks. Ha!

"I guess I should make that call," she said. It was definitely time to get out of here and go home. Wherever home was going to be tonight. She wasn't going to Haddon Hall. A fancy suite at the Drake wasn't right, either. She'd spent the day as a working girl. She should sleep like one, too. But that left her where?

"Here."

She jumped at the sound of his voice just behind

her. She turned to find him holding the phone. "Thank you."

"I'll leave you to your call."

The heat dropped twenty degrees the instant he shut the door behind him. At least it felt that way. She rested limply against his desk, staring at the phone but thinking about her new boss. There was no denying that he intrigued her. Tough enough to run a successful restaurant, soft enough to let his grandmother walk all over him.

The phone began to beep at her, and she jerked her thoughts to the problem at hand. She pressed the reset button and dialed information. After calling for a cab, she ran down a mental list of possibilities. They were dismally few and generally revolved around her platinum card. The friends she'd made at school were not close. Even if she felt comfortable enough to confide in any of them, which she didn't, there wasn't one of them she'd call at this hour of the morning.

A door banged in the hallway. Seconds later a taller, skinnier and somewhat younger version of Nick D'Angelo filled the doorway. He wore ratty black jeans that molded indecently to his long legs, an almost equally ratty T-shirt and a leather jacket.

"Now this is a nice if unexpected surprise," he said. "I was beginning to think old Niccolo was going monkish on me. So, who are you and why is my brother keeping you trapped in his office? I could rescue you, if you like." He extended his hand. "Joey

D'Angelo, knight in black leather." His grin was infectious.

Suddenly Sunny didn't feel quite so exhausted. What was it about D'Angelo men, anyway? She laughed. "I'm afraid my steed is already on its way. But thanks for the kind offer." She shook his hand.

He held on to her and bowed deeply. "Anytime, fair maiden." After pressing a warm kiss on the back of her hand, he released her and straightened. "And your name? My big brother doesn't ever get around to introducing most of his dates to the family. He has some strange idea that we scare the ladies off. Go figure."

"I'm not so certain he's afraid you'll scare them off so much as spirit them away."

His eyes widened in surprise. "A live one. Nice change, brother." He laughed. It was as engaging as his grin. It made Sunny wonder what Nick would be like if he loosened up a bit. But then, Joey didn't have the demands on him that Nick did.

"I like you...what did you say your name was?"

"I didn't. It's Sunny."

"Now there's a woman with intuitive parents. My folks? Joseph." He snorted. "Are you kiddin' me?" He shook his head. His dark hair was so short it didn't move. Another contrast with his brother. Interesting. She'd have figured Nick for the controlled short hair and Joey for the wilder, messier look.

Hmm. But more intrigue she didn't need. She was not about to get involved with the D'Angelo brothers.

"I think Joseph is a fine name," she said. "Very strong."

"Biblical. Yeah, yeah. I've heard it all."

She laughed. "Somehow I don't think you've let it slow you down all that much."

He shot her a mock sly grin. "I see my reputation precedes me." He moved closer. "So, exactly why *are* you in Nick's office?"

"I'm a new employee here and I was just making arrangements for a ride."

"Get out! Nick hired you?"

She raised an eyebrow. "Yes, he did. Why do you ask?"

"I like it when you get all ice princessy on me. Very nice. I bet that makes Nick nuts."

"I don't think much fazes your brother. And he hired me because you're leaving early for school."

He looked honestly chagrined by the reminder. "I know. But Mama Bennie and Nick understood. I just figured they'd find someone without having to advertise." He studied her a second. "Unless one of my cousins got married without me knowing, or you're Italian on your mother's side about six times removed."

She laughed again. "Nope. No Italian in my history."

Joey's grin returned. "Well, then, I guess my brother finally came to his senses."

"Actually, it was Mama Bennie who—"

Nick came into the office. "Sunny, your cab is— Hey, Joey." He caught his brother in an affectionate bear hug. "I thought you were already headed east."

"I was. But then Steve backed out on me." He turned to Sunny. "What a pal, huh? I mean, he agrees to sublet my apartment, then backs out on me when his girlfriend invites him to move in. I ask you, is that fair?"

"Perhaps she made a more tantalizing offer," Sunny teased. Then the light bulb went off in her head. "Hey, maybe I can help you out."

Nick stepped between them. "No." Gone was the easy affection he'd exuded moments ago.

"What do you mean, no?" Joey moved his brother behind him and pasted on a wide smile. "This is between me and the lady." He looked over his shoulder. "Unless perhaps you were planning on her stayin' at your place?"

"No!" When Sunny and Joey's eyes widened at his sudden vehemence, Nick frowned and tried again. "I mean, where she stays is none of my concern, as long as she reports to work on time."

Joey turned to Sunny. "Perfect. Because it will be hard for her to be late if she's sleeping right upstairs." He held out his hand. "Come on, I'll show you the place and we can talk terms."

Sunny blinked. "Upstairs? You live over the restaurant?"

"You bet. It's a great place. I even cleaned it up for Steve. The bum. Although I'm thinkin' now maybe I owe Steve, you know?" He hustled her from the office. Over his shoulder, he said, "Cancel the cab, Nick. She won't be needing it."

Nick responded by grabbing Joey's arm and dragging them both back to the doorway. "Hold on just a minute. She's only here short term. I'll find someone to rent your place. Just leave me a spare set of keys."

"Excuse me," Sunny said, extracting her arm from Joey's grip and moving between the two brothers. "I believe this is between Joseph and myself. Even if I don't remain under your employ, I will need a place to stay."

Joey chuckled. "Don't you just love it when she talks like that?"

Nick scowled. "Don't do this, Joey."

Joey was totally unaffected by his brother's demand. He shrugged. "Hey, you're the one who hired her."

Nick turned to Sunny. "Surely a Chandler can do better than renting a one-bedroom walk-up in this part of town."

Joey started to say something, but Sunny cut him off. "This Chandler will reside wherever she sees fit. And right at this moment, I think Joey's place sounds great. So, if you'll excuse us?"

Nick swore under his breath. "I knew this was going to be a huge mistake."

Joey punched his brother on the arm. "Lighten up, will ya? If she lasted a day with both you and Carlo on her case, she's already outlasted the first six women you hired for the kitchen. And they were your cousins."

Suddenly feeling better than she had all day, Sunny tossed Nick a victorious smile and allowed Joey to lead her to the back stairs.

4

SUNNY PRIED OPEN one eyelid, peered at the clock and groaned. It couldn't be time already. Surely she'd just fallen into bed minutes ago. Then she remembered. It was her day off. Her first in a week. She didn't have to rush out and run her errands before work. She had all afternoon. She might even put her errands off until evening. The idea of being off her feet for an entire day held an almost orgasmic appeal. She smiled sleepily and snuggled deeper beneath the covers.

Then shot dead upright when she heard a door banging open and people talking. *Inside* her apartment. Before she could wet her throat enough to call out, the invaders found her.

"Up and at 'em, sleepyhead. We need you. Father Sartori needs you. And you know the good father preaches patience better than he practices it." A tall, striking brunette stopped short in the doorway. "Well, surprise, surprise."

Sunny clutched the bedspread to her chest and pushed her hair from her face. "Um, who are you?" Had she been a little more awake, she'd have noticed the resemblance. But when the shorter, plumper woman pushed past the taller one, she knew without a doubt who had come calling. "Nick's sisters?"

That stopped the shorter one, who glanced at her taller sister with a speculative look in her eyes. "She said Nick, not Joey." They both turned their smiles to Sunny, who immediately understood what was going through their minds.

She shook her head. "No, no, you have it all wrong. I work for Nick. I'm the new kitchen help. Joey sublet me his apartment when his friend backed out. He's with Mama Bennie until Sunday, then he's going to school."

The taller one nodded approvingly. "Smart, concise and rational." She and her sister shared a laugh. "Definitely not Nick or Joey's type." She stepped forward and held out her hand. "Sorry to intrude on you like this, but since we have, I'm Marina." She shook Sunny's hand. "And this is my younger sister Andrea. And I might as well warn you, there are two more of us about to show up. Rachel and B.J., the younger ones, that is, except for Joey. He's the baby."

"In more ways than one," Andrea added, looking at the various posters on the walls. "I don't suppose he'll let you redecorate while you're here, will he?"

Sunny smiled. "With all that wonderful food I'm around all day, I figure staring at Heather Locklear and Elle MacPherson every night is a good thing. Keeps me on the straight and narrow."

"Definitely not Joey's type," Andrea agreed. "Well,

we'll get ourselves out of your bedroom now. We're all used to tramping in and out of each other's houses, but had we known—"

"We'd have at least knocked first," Marina finished with a smile. "And then barged in anyway." She wasn't in any apparent hurry to leave, however. "So, when did you start? Usually the D'Angelo grapevine works better than this, but with school just letting out and Cecelia's new baby finally home from the hospital and B.J. announcing she's expecting her second *and* third one early next year, it's been, well—"

"Normal," Andrea finished with a laugh.

Sunny felt like she was at a tennis match, her head was going back and forth so often. She wondered if they always completed each other's sentences. She couldn't imagine what it was like to grow up with so many siblings. Or any siblings, for that matter. Not for the first time, she felt a little pang of envy. "It must be wonderful to have that kind of support network." She didn't realize she'd spoken out loud until Marina answered.

"Yes, it is," she said without hesitation. "Of course, we never had the bathroom to ourselves, Nick and Papa Sal scared off most of our potential dates—it's a wonder any of us got married—and we had to live with Mama Bennie terrifying the teachers at conference time." Her smile softened. "But there was always someone to help you with your homework, and splitting the chores was a bit easier." She studied

Sunny with renewed interest. "I take it you didn't have those problems."

Sunny shook her head. "Well, I probably had an even harder time dating. Papa Sal and Nick combined would pale in comparison to my grandfather. But the housekeepers did the chores and my nanny helped me with my homework. And I had plenty of bathroom space." Her very own bathroom, in fact.

"Housekeepers and nannies?" Andrea sighed and sank into a chair. "Can I move in with your family? And bring my three kids with me?"

Marina sat on the end of the bed, making herself right at home. "With all that, why are you here? Since we're bonding and all," she added with a grin.

She really was gorgeous, Sunny thought. And Andrea was bright and pretty, as well. Both had thick, dark hair, shining brown eyes and beautiful skin. The D'Angelo genes were made of powerful stuff. All pale and blond, she should have felt lifeless next to such vibrancy. But somehow she didn't. There was no phoniness and no pretense with these two. She liked that. She liked that a lot.

"Actually, living here isn't that much different from my room at the sorority. Except we had different posters. I've adjusted pretty easily, and there's only one person to clean up after."

Marina and Andrea exchanged a look, then laughed. "We wouldn't know much about that, either. The sorority or only cleaning up after one person."

Sunny shrugged, but laughed with them. It had been a good week, better than she'd expected. She was dog tired, but it was a good tired. And she was already in love with the neighborhood. That part was very different from school or home. And she'd discovered she really enjoyed being on her own. Was thriving on it. The people were nice, and everything she needed was within walking distance.

She admitted to wanting to call home once or twice, just to let her grandparents know she was fine, but they knew where she was. She knew that because she'd spied Carl cruising down the street every so often in the limo. Edwin keeping an eye on her, no doubt. Well, that had worked to her advantage, too. She'd flagged Carl down the second time she'd seen him—thankful Edwin hadn't been in the back seat—and coerced him into getting one of the housekeepers to throw some of her things in a bag, then sneak it to her.

Other than that, she'd had no contact with her family. But then, she hadn't expected to. Neither Edwin nor Frances would give in. She was certain they were waiting for her to come crawling home so they could pass judgment on her immature decision. Well, they had a long wait coming.

"So, Nick hired you for the kitchen?" Andrea asked.

Marina shushed her sister, then turned to Sunny. "How long has it been?"

"A week. This is my first day off."

"Hey," Marina said, surprised. "A new world record. And you don't even speak Italian. Do you?"

Sunny smiled. "I'm learning. Quickly."

"I think I'm glad we barged in today." Andrea rubbed her hands. "We never can get enough information to use against our big brother. But this is too good. One week with both Nick and Carlo. You're either Wonder Woman or really desperate."

Sunny knew Andrea was fishing for information, but she realized she didn't mind. She'd spent too much of her life mingling with pretentious bores—admittedly her fault as much as her grandparents', as she'd suffered them in silence. She'd only just met Nick's sisters, but she knew without a doubt they'd never suffer through anything silently. Maybe she was mingling with the right people. The right people for her.

Marina crossed her legs. "So why work here?"

"It's a long story, but once I walked in the door and met Mama Bennie, I knew it was right."

"And after five minutes with Carlo?"

She laughed. "I was ready to quit. But only *after* committing homicide."

The sisters laughed and nodded in complete understanding, and Sunny knew she'd made two new friends. Friends of her own choosing. It was a ridiculously big moment for her, and she almost laughed at the absurdity of it.

"So why aren't we planning the wake?" Andrea asked.

She explained about her grandfather. Then added, "And Nick didn't think I could handle it, so I had that to prove, too." She shrugged at Marina's questioning lift of an eyebrow. "I am human."

"And female," Andrea said, her expression considering.

Sunny knew where Andrea was headed. "Yes, well, he's not hard on the eyes, that's for sure. But I'm not here to prove anything in that direction." So what if she'd caught him staring at her a few times, and it made things heat up in a way that had nothing to do with Italian cooking? She was on a mission to get a life, not a lover.

"Well, I still say you deserve some kind of award," Andrea said.

Sunny smiled. "A paycheck will suffice."

Marina grinned. "I think you're going to be a welcome addition. The women in this family have been providing all the entertainment for far too long now. It'll be fun being the audience for a change. Especially if you can give my big brother a run for his money. Do him good to learn all women don't swoon at the sight of his good looks." She studied Sunny again. "And you say you haven't swooned, right?"

Sunny blushed. She couldn't believe she was sitting almost naked in her own bed, talking to her new boss's sisters—women she'd just met—about her sex life. Or lack of one. "I definitely understand how he'd have a high swoon factor. But after this past week, I think we can safely say we see each other as points to be proven and nothing else."

Marina stood. "Well, the least you deserve is some rest." She stopped Sunny's protestation. "We've all done time in Nick's kitchen. Trust me, sleep when you can."

Andrea stood, as well. "We only have a few hours of reprieve, anyway. Rachel and B.J.'s husbands are watching the brood while we help Father Sartori with all the festival plans. And even double teaming them, you'd think we were asking them to sacrifice a kidney or something."

"I'm pretty sure John would be first in the donation line, given a choice," Marina joked. To Sunny, she added, "John is B.J.'s husband. He's a great guy, but with little Angelina being their only child and barely a toddler, he's still a bit terrified of children running in packs."

"Of course, with B.J. at the end of her second trimester and expecting twins, we saw it as our duty to help him get over his fears," Andrea added. "After all, in this family, he must be assimilated into the pack mentality if he hopes to survive."

Sunny felt a pang of commiseration for John. She

was only dealing with the two sisters, and it was all she could do to keep up. "Twins?"

"The first in the D'Angelo family."

"John is still adapting to the idea," Andrea added.

"Like he has a choice." Marina laughed. "Come on, we'd better get going. Leaving all the festival plans to the good father is never wise. Remember last time we left him in charge? He had Mrs. Amato running the ticket booth."

Andrea groaned. "She only speaks Italian, can't make change worth a hoot, is mostly deaf and sings all the time. Loudly. Off-key." She shuddered. "It was a nightmare. You're right, we better get over there."

Curiosity got the best of Sunny. "What festival are you helping with?"

"It's a summertime tradition in the neighborhood. Lots of music and games and dancing. And food. Enough to feed a small nation. Which is essentially what our neighborhood is, anyway," she said with a laugh. "It's three weeks away, but there's a ton still to do. D'Angelo's has been one of the caterers for this festival since it started over thirty years ago. The whole neighborhood pitches in with the decorations and such. Sometimes I think all the planning leading up to it is the true social occasion."

"With all the gossip going on, it's a wonder anything gets done." Andrea laughed.

"It sounds like a lot of fun," Sunny said. And it did.

Her social calendar had never included something as fun-sounding as this event. Quite the opposite.

Marina shuttled her sister out the bedroom door, but Andrea ducked her head back in. With a speculative gleam in her eye, she said, "We never turn down an extra pair of hands. Just ask Nick for directions. We'll be there until mid-afternoon at least. Or as long as the kids last after they get dropped off."

Marina nodded. "Hey, if you lasted a week in Nick's kitchen, this will be a breeze."

"Or send you screaming back to wherever you came from," Andrea added with a laugh. "Come if you dare."

"I don't think I'm running anywhere just yet. Let me shower and get dressed and I'll be there. If it's okay. I'm not really a resident."

Marina's eyebrows rose, and she really looked like her brother. "You pay rent, do you not? This is your mailing address, is it not? We're like a village here, made up of decades of immigrants." She shrugged. "What can I say? We are more open-minded than our ancestors, perhaps, but we still stick together. Show us what you're made of. You'll get a fair shake."

Andrea agreed. "You won't know unless you try."

Marina smiled. "I'll give you some advice. Good gossip is a great way to get in."

"I don't have any gossip."

"You have the story about how a blond-haired rich girl got hired by Nick D'Angelo, to work in Carlo's kitchen, no less. That will get you in the door. Trust me." She winked. "After that, it's all up to you."

"That is, if you still want to try after stepping into this madness," Andrea warned as they headed out.

"Welcome to the neighborhood, Sunny," Marina called, then the front door slammed shut.

Sunny flopped back in bed. She'd just survived Hurricane D'Angelo. She didn't feel sleepy. In fact, she felt invigorated. *Enough to go stand on your feet on your day off?* She thought of the two women she'd just met, their vivacity and the natural energy that emanated from them. She wanted to be a part of that.

She'd wanted a life of her own choosing. Never in her wildest imagination would she have chosen this one. But somehow it had chosen her. And she found she liked it.

"Grandfather, if you could only see your little CEO now."

5

Sunny stopped in front of the office door, hesitating before knocking. She'd been hoping Mama Bennie would be around so she wouldn't have to bug Nick for directions to Father Sartori's. No such luck. She knocked.

"Yeah?"

"It's Sunny. I just have a quick question."

"Come in."

His tone was sharp, but she'd been around him long enough to distinguish between anger and distraction. It hadn't taken a week for her to realize that running even a small restaurant like D'Angelo's was one monstrous list of never-ending tasks. She'd been amazed at what he was responsible for and wasn't sure how he kept it all under control. She poked her head in the door. His dark head was bent over his desk. He didn't look up.

He wasn't wearing his usual white button-down shirt with the sleeves rolled up. He was wearing a faded Chicago Bears T-shirt, and his hair was more tousled than usual, as if he'd been raking his fingers through it. Often.

She ignored the itch in her fingertips and slipped into the room. "I need some directions. Marina and Andrea said I should ask you."

He had been punching numbers almost viciously into a calculator, but stopped instantly and looked up. "What did you just say?"

"Marina and Andrea asked me to join them today, and I need directions to Father Sartori's. They said to ask you."

"Why are you going out with my sisters?" he asked, giving her a suspicious look.

"They invited me. Just this morning."

"You don't even know my sisters."

She smiled. "Not all of them, but I know two of them now."

"Since when?"

"Since they barged into my bedroom this morning, thinking I was Jocy."

Nick stared at her for a full ten seconds, then tossed his pencil on the desk and leaned back in his chair. "Oh, that's just great."

Sunny propped her hands on her hips. "Well, thank you so very much." Maybe being an only child wasn't so bad, after all.

"You have no understanding of what this means for me."

"This really has nothing to do with you." She turned to leave. "I'll find it on my own. Maybe Mr. Bertolucci down at the grocery can help me."

"Wait."

She paused and glanced back.

"I'm sorry I snapped. It's been a bitch of a morning, and the inventory Joey did before he left isn't adding up. Sometimes I wonder where that boy's head is when it isn't buried neck deep in some computer programming code."

"Judging by the posters on the wall of his bedroom, I could hazard a guess," Sunny said with a dry smile.

She thought his mouth twitched at the corners, but she couldn't be certain. She knew he had a killer smile, though it had never been aimed at her. She had seen him with the patrons, charm turned on full blast. And quite a powerful blast it was. He was good at what he did, and people obviously loved him.

"If you can hang on about ten minutes, I'll take you to Father Sartori's myself."

She told herself it was shock from his offer, not panic, that filled her. "No, that's okay. I know you're busy. Just give me a general idea. I'll find it. I have a good head for directions."

He was studying her openly. Her panic button remained in the engaged position. It was one thing to intercept a look now and then and torment herself with the possibility that there might be something behind it. But this was direct and challenging.

"What kind of head do you have for columns and figures?"

"Huh?" It took her a second to process the question. She almost laughed. Here she was, wondering if her boss had the hots for her body, when in fact he was really interested in her mind. Oh, the irony. She hid her smile. "Um, actually I'm pretty good with columns and figures."

Nick shoved himself out of his chair. "Great. Can you tally columns five and six for me, and then match them to column nine? I've got to unload a few more things in the back, then we can get out of here." He brushed past her but didn't seem to feel the same full-body electrical zap she did. "I really appreciate it." Then he was gone.

Sunny crossed to his chair and sat down. It was still warm from his body. She looked at the jumbled disarray he called a desk and wondered that he got anything done at all.

Her grandfather would have had a heart attack at Nick's lack of organizational skills. And she was apparently enough of her grandfather's little girl to be equally disgusted by it. The same fingers that had itched to weave through his hair itched to straighten his desk. But she resisted. She wasn't here to run his company or tell him how to run his company. Although, if he was interested, she had one or two ideas.

Studying the books in front of her, she sighed. The columns were on wide, light green spreadsheets, pressed into what looked like an old leather binder. She didn't think they made these anymore. "Wonder if he's heard of that great new invention," she muttered. "The computer."

She began to punch numbers and almost immediately spotted where Joey made his mistake. He'd transposed two numbers. She corrected them and circled the two matching totals on the calculator tape in red. Then, curious, she scanned the other columns, and found several more errors. Ten minutes later she'd made changes on five pages and saved her boss several hundred dollars. She considered searching further, but was hesitant to do it without asking first. She went to find Nick.

She stepped into the small stockroom, but her mouth went dry before she could speak. Nick was bent at the waist, facing away from her, prying open a small wooden crate. Jeans. She'd never seen him in jeans. Especially not ones that showcased his backside and thighs quite so, um, amazingly well. She must have made a sound—probably strangling on her own libido—because he straightened and turned to face her.

"Couldn't figure it out? Never mind, just leave it and I'll look at it again later when the numbers aren't swimming before my eyes."

Sunny enjoyed the smug smile that curved her lips. "No problem. Error found and corrected. In fact, I found a couple. I paper-clipped the calculator tape to the pages I fixed. You know, you really need a computer. I could have you set up in a heartbeat." He had yet to reply, and her confidence faltered a bit. Had she gone too far? She gestured to the shelves. "So. Need any help back here? Although I must insist on clocking in if you say yes."

The tension left his face, and she could almost see him relax the bunched muscles in his shoulders and arms. Muscles that bunched right back up, and very nicely, too, when he folded his arms across his chest. "You must insist?" He mimicked her stilted tone. Did she really sound like that?

There was a light in his eyes, sending a warning. Sunny wasn't certain what that warning meant. "It's...just that it's my day off."

"And you plan to spend it working free for Father Sartori."

"I thought it would be fun."

Nick finally did what he hadn't all week. He smiled directly at her. She thought, a bit faintly, that perhaps it hadn't been a good idea to provoke him, after all.

"More fun than helping me unpack olive oil?"

Her reaction to that made no sense whatsoever. The man owned a restaurant, after all, and olive oil was part of his business. So why images of entirely different and wholly inappropriate uses for olive oil flashed into her head was beyond her. She'd probably blush every time Carlo handed her a bottle of it from now on. How mortifying.

"I—I'm guessing yes." She finally looked away from his penetrating gaze. "Marina and Andrea made it sound like something I'd like to be involved in."

"Marina and Andrea could give Tom Sawyer and Dennis the Menace a run for their money."

"So you don't think the festival is fun?"

"Oh, it's quite an event. A great deal of fun is had by many. But for me, it's work. Enjoyable work, but work nonetheless."

"Marina said that D'Angelos has helped cater the festival since it started."

"You and my sisters had quite the chat, didn't you?"

Remembering it, Sunny couldn't help but smile. "Well, it wasn't the traditional way to meet new friends, but we seemed to hit it off."

The smile faded, and the wariness returned. "What exactly are your plans, Sunny? Now you're getting chummy with my family and getting involved in neighborhood doings. Is this some sort of social-boundary-expanding vacation for you?"

Her mouth dropped open, then quickly snapped shut. "My idea of a vacation, expanding or not, does not include working twelve-hour days, being violently shouted at in Italian, soaking my aching feet in hot water every night and drifting off to la-la land with visions of Heather Locklear's boobs in my head." She stepped forward, realizing full well he could fire her on the spot but not caring at the moment. "My reasons for being here are my own. I show up for work, do my job responsibly and earn the right to do whatever I want with my day off, including working for Father Sartori and socializing with anyone I care to, including your sisters. I happen to like making my own friends, choosing my daily agenda with no help from anyone else and going wherever I damn well please without having to file my itinerary with a driver." She was almost nose to chin with him. "If you have a problem with my work ethic or job performance, then by all means let me know. Otherwise, I'd appreciate it if you'd keep your suspicions to yourself. Your sisters, if you haven't noticed, are grown women, also used to making their own choices." She spun around to leave. "I went from one domineering, controlling male to another," she muttered. "I just want a nice quiet life, a few good friends and a challenging job. What is so wrong with that? It shouldn't be that hard."

She was as quickly spun around by Nick to face him, but he immediately dropped his hand from her arm. "Wait a minute."

"Am I fired?"

"Not yet."

"Then I'm out of here until tomorrow."

"Sunny, will you wait a damn minute? I'm trying to apologize."

She stopped. "For that, I have a minute. Possibly two." She eyed him. "Go ahead."

He grinned. Grinned!

"Wait!" He lifted a hand when she scowled and moved to leave again. "I can't help it. You're probably going to hate this, but you're cute when you're mad."

"Oh, okay, that was low. If I'm not fired, I should just quit."

"Don't." He exhaled heavily on a frustrated sigh and shoved his fingers through his hair, drawing her attention yet again to his luxuriant tousled locks. She weakened. Just slightly, but that dip in her knees was most definitely there. Damn him and her itchy fingertips.

"I don't know why I got so worked up at the idea of you being with my sisters," he said. "Actually, I do. My sisters have a history of making my life as miserable as possible. I thought they'd be too caught up in their own daily dramas to find time to make my life hell, but now that they've discovered you... Well, you'll have to forgive my little panic attack, but trust me when I say it was well deserved."

Sunny found the remainder of her anger fleeing, replaced by honest curiosity. "What could your sisters possibly do with me that would threaten you in any way?"

His gaze narrowed. "They're married. All four of them. And as of one month ago, they all four have children. It's some kind of contagious disease, and they think everyone should share it with them. I didn't want them spreading the germ to you."

"I'm not sure, but I think I'm insulted."

Nick's lips quirked slightly. "No insult intended. I'm just not the marrying kind. I'm married to my job. Perhaps I should have just warned you right off and left it at that."

"Who says *I'm* the marrying kind? And if I was, why do you assume I would find *you* appropriate?" She'd been aiming to make a dent in his inflated ego. Apparently she needed bigger ammo than a mere snub. All she had gotten was an amused smile. But at a momentary flash of something...predatory in his eyes, she backed off and cleared her throat. "I'm just saying that I'm not interested in anyone right now, either. I merely enjoyed your sisters' company and thought it sounded like a way to get to know my new neighborhood and neighbors a bit better."

"You're still on probation here, you know."

"I know. But I like living here and, job at D'Angelos or not, I plan to stick around for a while." He looked concerned. She smiled at the minor victory. "So I guess you'd better get used to the idea."

NICK FOUND HIMSELF looking up for the umpteenth time that afternoon, his gaze falling unerringly on one Sunny Chandler. She'd charmed the clerical collar off Father Sartori within minutes of meeting him, explaining that she wasn't Catholic but admiring the artistry of the stained glass and statuary in such a way as to give the father plenty of time to show off his beloved domain. Mr. Fabricio had fallen victim next when she'd tried out her newly learned Italian with the old-world shoe repairman.

Nick scowled. Pale and blond, with her willowy body and finely boned face, she stuck out like a cool diamond dropped into a collection of vibrant costume jewelry. And yet somehow, amazingly, she'd begun to find her way in.

Not that everyone had welcomed her with open arms. Mrs. Trotta was a bit miffed. But then, Mrs. Trotta had been trying, unsuccessfully, to marry all three of her daughters off to Nick. Actually—he glanced around—there were more than a few mamas unamused with the new arrival. He enjoyed that for a moment, but found his gaze straying once again to Sunny. She was supposed to be a temporary employee. She was not supposed to insinuate herself into his life. Personal or public.

He thought about what she'd said, that she'd only wanted to get to know her neighbors. That this had nothing to do with him. Well, she didn't understand small neighborhoods. She would have everything to do with him, whether she wanted to or not. Because, for every one unamused mama out there, there were other mamas who'd love nothing more than to see him married. To anyone. Maybe especially an outsider. Then they could appease their wounded egos that he hadn't chosen their daughters because he thought he was too good for them and see, they'd been right all along!

Which couldn't be further from the truth. Yes, he tended to date women from outside the neighborhood. But that wasn't because he didn't love Italian women. Not that he felt he had to date someone with a shared heritage—especially as he wasn't planning to marry any of them—but he was naturally attracted to women who just happened to fit the profile. Voluptuous, dark-haired, sloe-eyed women who knew how to enjoy their own bodies...and his.

He only dated outside the neighborhood so he could keep some modicum of his private life private. Those mamas looking to see him married would have a long wait...and would have to look a whole lot farther than one Sunny Chandler. She was the most uptight, overconfident, prim-lipped...blonde he'd ever met. Not to mention she failed sorely in the voluptuous department.

Nope. She wasn't even a candidate for the Nick D'Angelo dating pool.

He tore his gaze away from her as she laughed at something Andrea said, but not before her eyes met his for a split second. Her smile faltered, and he found himself glancing back. But she was once again engaged by some story Andrea was telling. His gaze lingered as he tried to puzzle out his preoccupation with her.

"You finished here?"

He looked up to find Mr. Fabricio's grandson Tony standing next to him. He glanced at the list of supplies he'd been making and shook his head. Mostly in self-disgust. He really had to get his mind back on work.

"Father Sartori can't decide how many tables we should have this year."

Nick nodded. "I'm coming." He purposely didn't look at Sunny as he stood and shoved the half-formed list in his back pocket. But he wanted to.

Tony ran ahead, leaving Nick to follow at a slower pace as he forced himself to think only about tables. Last year there had been too many, and it had inhibited dancing. But the year before that, it had been hot and they'd run out of places for the older people to sit early on. It was supposed to be a hot summer, so this would take some planning.

Hot summer. A hot summer with a cool blonde.

He swore under his breath and pushed into the shadowy interior of the church. His skin cooled off, but even the spiritual surroundings did little to cool the steady emergence of his libido.

When Sunny's probation was up, she'd have to go, he abruptly decided. It was the only solution. He wasn't getting his work done, at least not as smoothly as he usually did. And she was no small wrinkle.

Father Sartori and two other men were arguing at the back of the church. Mrs. Delatorre looked up from the pew she was occupying and sent him a knowing smile. He sighed. He had enough wrinkles. Sunny had to go. It was either that or he'd end up in bed with her.

He hadn't let himself even think that, but now that he had, he realized the idea had been lurking in his subconscious all along. Mrs. Delatorre scooted her ample body from the end of the pew, knelt and made the sign of the cross, then smiled at him again before leaving.

Nick felt his skin heat, as if she'd known his thoughts had strayed to the less than pure. But now that they were there, he decided to give them a shot. Why not? Nothing else had worked. He smiled. What if they did go to bed? Would she run home to Grandfather? Probably. He'd get this sudden weird fixation with her out of his system and get her out of his life as well.

The more he thought about it, the more the idea took root. It was certainly more enjoyable—for both of them—than simply firing her. Which, as it stood, he had no basis for. But she wouldn't stay around after they'd gone to bed together. She was too high-society for an affair with him, and he was too neighborhood for the likes of her.

He didn't feel dishonorable about the whole thing, either. They were both adults, and it wasn't like he was planning on forcing her into anything. Sure, she worked for him, but she didn't depend on her paycheck, and therefore him, for her survival. No, she had a reason for being here, but it wasn't because she needed her job. She certainly wasn't worried about keeping it, considering how she'd spoken to him earlier. At the very least, they were on equal footing from a man-woman standpoint. If she wanted to say no and keep working for him, she would.

But after some of the looks he'd intercepted this past week, he didn't think she'd say no. It might take a while to melt the ice, but he realized that while he usually had little patience for that sort of thing, with Sunny it could prove...well, exciting.

All he had to do was get her to take a little walk on the wild side with him. They would both have a good time...and then get on with their lives.

6

NICK LEFT his office and trudged toward the kitchen. It had been a rough week, and it was about to get even rougher. He was not looking forward to his imminent confrontation with Carlo. He had enough problems. The truckers were striking, and a nasty flu bug had wiped out half the serving staff for almost a week, putting a major damper on his plans to seduce Sunny. He remembered now why he never had relationships that lasted very long. The restaurant business was a very demanding mistress. For the first time, he found himself resenting that a bit.

Which made no sense at all. His planned fling with Sunny would certainly be no more important than any other fling he'd ever had, which was to say not important at all. Besides, with things the way they were, he needed Sunny in the kitchen more than he needed her in his bed. Giving her any reason to leave would not be a wise business move.

The huge neighborhood wedding D'Angelos was catering, as well as the influx of summer patrons in the restaurant, had added to the chaos. They'd put in long hours of overtime, but there hadn't been even a minute of personal time alone with her.

At least the kids were out of school for the summer. That meant his meddling sisters couldn't come in and help him out. Much as he needed the extra hands, he didn't need the extra mouths. Not their mouths, anyway. Mama Bennie enjoyed keeping him informed, in the guise of family news, of course. But he'd seen the look in her eyes and had had serious second thoughts about his take-Sunny-to-bed plans. If Mama Bennie or his sisters got one whiff of a liaison between them, no matter how brief, their matchmaking plans would go into warp drive.

It had been ridiculous to think he could plan a date, much less a major seduction, especially now.

He pushed into the kitchen to give Carlo the news that the produce would be late—a surefire way to start everyone's day off with a very loud bang—and ran headlong, or body long, into Sunny.

"Ooh!" She backed up immediately and turned sideways to allow him to pass. "Sorry, didn't see the door move until it was too late."

"That's okay." But it wasn't. That innocent brush against the damp, stained apron she had tied around her too-skinny frame had his body all in an uproar.

This was a sign. He should stay the hell away from her. She didn't belong here. He knew that, and he was positive she knew it, as well.

"I've got to talk to Carlo," he said firmly. No nonsense, pure business. That was the way to handle any encounters with her. "The produce won't be here on time."

The look of horror on her face mirrored his feelings exactly.

"You might want to take a break," he added, bending a little. Okay, a lot. Damn, but she was pretty with her cheeks all flushed like that. She looked more touchable, more approachable. He put another few inches between them. "Why don't you go outside. Where you won't hear the screaming."

"I could go down to Mr. Fabricio's and not be far enough away for that." She lifted one eyebrow in that way she had that totally intrigued him. Very...regal looking. Which should put him a mile off, but instead made him fight to keep his distance.

"What is it about Italians and swearing anyway?" she asked, sounding serious.

"It's an art form we take delight in elevating to new heights."

She folded her arms, and he struggled not to look at how the act emphasized the shape of her small breasts pressing against the heavy cotton apron. What, had he regressed to high school here? All leering looks and drooling fantasies?

The simple, sad answer was yes, apparently he had. He tried to ignore it.

"So I've observed," she said.

He wondered idly if she realized how she sounded.

If she realized how badly he wanted to shake up that poise of hers, hear her get a bit throaty, a bit rough, demanding— He stopped right there.

"At least you're getting exposure to another culture," he responded steadily. "Consider it educational."

Her prim little mouth curved ever so slightly at the corners. He'd never wanted to taste anything so badly in his life.

"While I'm thrilled to have the opportunity to learn another language," she said, "the fact that eighty percent of what I've learned can't be repeated in mixed company—or any company, for that matter—has diminished my sense of accomplishment somewhat."

Nick caved in and grinned. It was that or grab her and yank her into his arms. She stood there, tendrils of hair plastered to her flushed cheeks, sauce stains on her chin, hands reddened from all the time spent in dishwater...sounding every bit like a dissatisfied country-club matron at a luncheon. "Well, you can use them all you want in my kitchen."

She favored him with a smile in return. "How enchanting." She sidled by him, careful not to brush against him.

The door swung behind her, and he struggled against the impulse to follow her. He told himself it was because he'd do anything to avoid dealing with Carlo. It was not because he wanted to see the midday breeze cool the heat from her cheeks. It was only when his fingers began to cramp that he realized he'd curled them into his palms to fight the urge to brush away the damp strands of hair that had escaped her hair net.

He squared his shoulders and turned resolutely to the kitchen where Carlo awaited him. Perhaps dealing with his head chef was the safer bet, after all.

SUNNY PAUSED outside the kitchen doors and found herself glancing inside as they swung closed. Nick stood where he'd been, body rigid, hands clenched, looking lost in thought.

Probably trying to figure out how to tell Carlo about the produce in a way that would cause the fewest dish replacement orders, she thought. She admitted she'd found herself staring at him far too often, bringing down the wrath of Carlo every time she'd gotten caught with head in the clouds instead of hot, soapy dishwater.

She'd wondered often that first week why Nick kept such a temperamental chef. Then she'd tasted Carlo's Veal Parmesan and knew. Nick had assured her that Carlo was fairly typical of his breed—genius chef. Besides, he was a second cousin. Family came first.

Still, she was amazed at the number of people who claimed the same D'Angelo heritage. She'd been invited to visit his sisters twice this week. Both times she'd left feeling like a shell-shocked war veteran. Dazed, with her ears ringing from the constant noise.

Yet she'd go back again. With enthusiasm.

Nick had never said another word about her budding friendship with his family. Actually, until five minutes ago, Nick hadn't said two words to her that weren't directly work-related. She realized she'd felt a bit miffed about that. She wasn't used to being background material.

She gave a self-deprecating laugh as she rubbed her back and moved down the hall toward the bathrooms. "What a self-centered little socialite you are, after all, Miss Chandler," she muttered dryly. She hated to admit it, but her grandfather had been at least partially right about how far removed she was from the real day-to-day grind.

Well, she was a stranger to it no more. The past week had tested her commitment to her new life in ways her first seven days of servitude hadn't. But all the times she felt overworked and underappreciated had been balanced by the fact that Nick was certainly more of both. The man slaved right along with the rest of them, and more often then not, when she dragged herself upstairs at one in the morning, his office light was still on.

For all that she felt pride in sticking it out, she knew she didn't have half the drive Nick did. And that was because his business, his family, meant something to him. They claimed a part of his soul. They were his passion. How was she going to make it at Chandler Enterprises if she didn't have that inside her?

Despite her fatigue, she'd spent the past several nights lying awake until close to dawn, trying to decide what to do if he kept her on after her month was up. The kitchen of D'Angelos was not her future. Yet, while the boiling environs—both in temperature and temperament—of the restaurant business didn't speak to her soul, neither did the cold environs of Chandler Enterprises.

Which left her precisely where?

She liked the neighborhood—the shops, the people who ran them. The noise, the smells, the warmth. It was so different from anything she'd known, and yet a part of her had cleaved to that warmth immediately and fully. Her former life felt more sterile now that she had this to compare it to. And for all Marina's talk that Sunny's background would make her an outsider here, Sunny really hadn't felt that at all.

She pushed into the bathroom, dampened a paper towel and held it to her flushed cheeks. Nick had been right about them, though. No matter what she told his sisters to the contrary, everyone from his nieces and nephews to the corner baker had her and Nick matched up.

She paused while rubbing her skin, recalling the brief moment when she'd collided with Nick. What if part of her new life included a little fling? A fling with a real man. Not the dried-up, corporate-ladder climbers her grandfather relentlessly matched her up with.

Nick D'Angelo was definitely all real man.

She fanned her newly heated cheeks. Boy, was he ever.

But how could she have a fling with him and work

for him, as well? So what were her options? She could find another job that might be more suitable to her and stay in the neighborhood. But what job could she take? She hadn't a clue.

She left the bathroom and winced at the sudden voluble argument that erupted behind the kitchen door. Maybe she would go outside for a few minutes, after all.

She spied the sign for the festival as she went out the back door. It was two weeks away. The same weekend her probation period would finally end.

Attending the festival would be her reward to herself for sticking it out. And also her deadline for deciding what the next step in her new life would be.

If it included staying in the neighborhood a while longer, would it also include trying to get one Niccolo D'Angelo into bed?

RUBBING HIS FACE, Nick looked at the clock on his office wall. One forty-five in the morning. He groaned when his back protested as he moved in his chair. It had been a hell of a long day. But Carlo hadn't quit, they'd somehow survived until the produce truck showed up...and he'd been too blessedly busy to think about Sunny.

Much.

He might not have had any time alone with her, but with him pulling triple duty waiting tables and helping out in the kitchen, they'd been almost on top of each other all evening long. His body, tired as it was, got aroused each time he thought of her. Apparently there was no such thing as being too tired to want Sunny. If there was, he'd have reached that zenith hours ago.

He heard a noise in the hallway. With surprising speed, he stood and crossed to the door before giving his actions too much thought. Sunny was passing on her way to the back stairs.

"Hey."

She jumped, then turned, a hand pressed to her heart. "I'm sorry, you startled me."

Her hair was a damp mat against her head, barely held in place by her sliding hair net. Her cheeks were more pale than flushed, and her eyes were dull from fatigue. He wasn't sure who he resented more in that moment, her for taking on a job she had no business being in or him for letting her work herself to the bone.

"Is something wrong?" she asked.

"No, I just..." Something flickered in her eyes. If he wasn't mistaken, it was...hope? "I know I've worked you really hard this week, but it is appreciated."

The flicker died. "As long as your appreciation shows up in my paycheck."

"Do you really need the money?" He held up his hand when anger flashed in her eyes. "I'm really not trying to pry. It's just that I can't help but wonder. I mean, we both know you're not meant for this lifestyle."

She folded her arms and leaned against the far wall. "And just what lifestyle *am* I meant for?"

"Did your family cut you off or something?"

She continued to stare at him.

"Okay, okay, so it's none of my business. I just hate to see you so worn out."

"And if I'd stayed home with my granddaddy and grandmommy, I could be dallying about in a life of ease right now instead of doing an honest day's work? Is that what you're saying?"

He shook his head and raked his fingers through his hair. "Obviously I'm more tired than you are, because I'm not handling this remotely well. Go on up to bed. I'll see you tomorrow. If Tina and Roberto come back on tomorrow, maybe I can shift one of them to the kitchen for a few hours and give you some time off."

"Not necessary," she said sharply. "As long as I get my day off on Monday, that'll do." She moved away from the wall, and his hand was on her arm, stopping her, before he even realized it.

She turned and looked from his hand to his face, surprise in her eyes.

He let go, but he was surprised, too, at how reluctant he was to do so. He couldn't deny he wanted to follow her upstairs to bed. And not for sex. That alone shocked him into backing up a step. This need he felt to tuck her into bed, maybe stroke her face until the exhaustion was smoothed away a bit, watch her fall asleep...definitely wrong. Wanting Sunny—when he allowed himself to think that way—was supposed to be all about sex, about pleasure. Nothing more.

"You'll...you'll get paid. On time. With a bonus for all the extra hours," he said, stepping inside his office.

She nodded, but her gaze stayed on his.

He wondered what she was thinking. What she was wanting. Him?

"Good night," he said, his voice deeper, rougher. Fatigue, he told himself. He needed to sleep, was all.

She paused, and his heart began to kick up. Apprehension? Or anticipation?

"Good night," she said softly.

His simultaneous relief and disappointment told him it had been both. He made a mental note to call in a few more reinforcements tomorrow. He had to spend less time in the kitchen with Sunny.

He stayed in the hall and listened to her footsteps as she climbed the stairs. He was still standing there, lost in thought, when the springs squeaked as she settled into her bed. Didn't it figure that Joey's bedroom was directly above his office? He swore under his breath and reluctantly went back to work.

7

"SO, WHAT are you going to wear?" Andrea flopped on the bed, then oomphed when her four-year-old daughter leaped on top of her. "Callie, Mommy doesn't want to play trampoline right now." The bright, dark-haired little girl giggled and jumped on her again. Andrea gave a mock roar, rolled her daughter onto her back and wrestled until they were both laughing too hard to continue.

Sunny turned to her closet, smiling. Andrea was great with her kids. So were all Nick's sisters. She'd never really given any thought to her future where kids were concerned. Lately, however, she'd begun to.

"What am I wearing?" Sunny laughed and stared in her closet. Her wardrobe had changed. Dramatically. The clothes she'd had Carl deliver what seemed like a lifetime ago hung unworn in her closet. How had she ever thought her staid designer clothes would be suitable here? And those were the casual clothes she'd worn in college.

Nick's sisters had taken her shopping after her first paycheck. That was the day Sunny had discovered the thrill of bargain shopping. In fact, she was quite proud of how she'd applied her business acumen to making her paycheck stretch. Yes, she had a platinum card, and she'd used it precisely once. To pay Joey that first month's rent in advance. From then on she'd been determined to make it solely on her own. And she had, she thought, as she fingered the bright red sundress she'd gotten yesterday. Pride filled her as she turned to Andrea.

"I'm not attending the wedding. I'm working in food prep, so I'm pretty sure that means the standard black pants and white jacket." She turned and held the white jacket against her chest. "A real fashion statement, don't you think?"

Andrea sat her daughter on her lap and began fixing her pigtails. "Well, there is always after the wedding."

Sunny sighed. There was no use trying to get Andrea off her matchmaking kick. And, if she'd admit it, lately she'd had a hard time getting her own mind off of it. She'd given a lot of thought to her fling idea. Nick's comment last week about her not fitting in had stung more than a little, mostly because he'd been right.

"Is Nick driving you to the ceremony?"

Sunny rolled her eyes in exasperation. "You just don't give up, do you?" She pulled on a white cotton T-shirt, pulled the starched jacket over it and buttoned it up. "This is not a date. There is no dating."

Andrea's daughter looked at her. "Don't you like my Uncka Nicco?"

Sunny's smile caught but held. She knelt in front of the dimpled little girl. "Everyone loves your Uncka Nicco. He's my boss and I have a great deal of respect for him." She looked above Callie's head directly at Andrea. "But that's all there is and ever will be between us."

Andrea opened her mouth, but Sunny stared her into closing it again. However, her aggravating little smile told Sunny she hadn't given up. Sunny swallowed a groan and stepped into the little bathroom to pin her hair up under the hairnet.

"Speaking of your uncle," she heard Andrea say, "why don't you go on downstairs and see if he's ready to leave." Callie scampered out, and Andrea came to lean in the bathroom doorway. She looked at Sunny's mirrored reflection. "Why?"

For once, she wasn't teasing or pushing. Sunny turned and pulled the last bobby pin from between her lips. She jammed it in her bun and answered honestly. "I won't be here forever, Andrea. Nick is right. This isn't my life."

Andrea was smart enough not to be insulted. Sunny had made it clear often how much admiration she had for all the D'Angelo family had accomplished.

That didn't stop Andrea from folding her arms,

however, and settling firmly against the door frame. "So?"

Sunny's mouth dropped open, then she shut it. "So, I can't believe you really want to keep thrusting me at your brother when you know damn well nothing can come of it."

"Oh? There's a law now forbidding rich girls from marrying self-made men from the other side of town?"

Sunny's gaze narrowed. "Unfair. You know it's not about money. It's more than cultural differences. You know what I face going back to. How in the world would I ever combine my life with his? Even if I found a way, he'd hate my world." She pushed gently past Andrea and sat on her bed to put on her shoes. "*I* hate my world. And why am I even talking like I'm marrying the guy in the first place?"

Andrea sat next to her and put her arm around Sunny's waist. "Yeah," she said, smiling deeply when Sunny looked at her. "Why are you? Hmm?"

Sunny dropped her chin to her chest and sighed.

Andrea rubbed her shoulder. "We wouldn't push if we didn't think the two of you were already so attracted to one another that everyone can practically see the sparks fly."

Sunny gave Andrea the eyebrow lift.

Andrea shrugged. "Okay, so maybe we would have pushed a little. But we're not stupid. Nick has no trouble getting women. It's not like we're trying to fix up a hopeless case here. But there's just something about the two of you—"

Sunny took Andrea's hand in both of her own. "I won't lie. I'm attracted, okay? Obviously you know that."

"He is, too."

Sunny wondered about that. She didn't intercept as many looks as she had, or thought she had, earlier on. But every once in a while she'd catch him staring and... She shook that thought off. "Even so, I have a lot of things to figure out right now."

Andrea was only a year older than Sunny, but the wisdom in her eyes was ageless. "There is no bad time to fall in love, Sunny. Ask yourself which you'd regret more when you're eighty. Turning your back on a job, a place to live? Or a man who might be the one you'll share your whole life with? If it doesn't work out, at least you know. Walk away, and you'll never know."

Before Sunny could respond, Callie came bounding into the room. "It's time to go!"

Andrea scooped her daughter up and swung her high, making her squeal. "Then we'd better go!" They left the apartment with laughter and more squeals in their wake, leaving Sunny to wander behind them, lost in thoughts she'd rather not be having.

NICK FOUND his attention wandering to the bride and groom more often than necessary. The reception was going smoothly. Or as smoothly as these things tended to go. But the wine was flowing freely and the band was playing and people weren't so concerned that there had been more cannoli than napoleons.

"They look happy, don't you think?"

Nick turned to find B.J. standing next to him. "As much as this shindig costs, they'd better be happy or I'll hear from Mrs. Costanza about it."

B.J. laughed. "Well, silly me for thinking you might see more than dollar signs in this thing. I don't even know why I try. You're not exactly the sentimental type."

Oddly, that assessment stung. It shouldn't have— she was completely correct. "I'm sentimental about some things," he protested. At her questioning look, he thought for a moment and said, "I always wear my Bears jersey during home games."

She smacked him on the shoulder, and they both laughed. But her words stayed with him.

He found his gaze straying to Sunny as she hustled out with another tray of champagne glasses. He could all but feel his sister's speculative gaze, so he turned to her and gave her a quick hug. "Thanks for pitching in today." He nodded to her middle. "How're the bambinos today?"

The most serene smile crossed her face as her hand drifted to her belly. "I think they're in training for the WWF. But so far, they're welterweights." She grinned at him. "Ask me again in another month and I'm sure I'll be giving you an earful."

On impulse, he kissed her cheek. "You'll do fine, Barbara Jean. You're a wonderful mother. And don't worry, John will catch up to speed. Or I'll catch him up for you."

He'd meant it as a joke but was shocked to see tears spring to his baby sister's eyes. "Oh, Niccolo." She suddenly flung her arms around him and hugged him. "I take back what I said. So what if you're stubborn and won't see what's right in front of your nose. As a brother, you're not too bad. Most of the time."

"Gee, thanks." He hugged her. Pregnancy hormones. His sisters had been pregnant often enough that he knew it was best to smile and nod and hug a lot.

She punched him on the shoulder even as she kissed his cheek.

"Ow! Hey! What'd I do to deserve that?"

She smiled sweetly as she turned to walk away. "That's to keep you on your toes. Wake up, Nick, and smell the bridal bouquet. Our family heritage is more about this—" she patted her belly "—than this." She nodded toward the long banquet display tables. "Without one, what's the point of working so hard for the other?"

Nick opened his mouth to reply, but she was gone. *Pregnant women.*

"I think that about does it."

He turned to find Sunny standing behind him. Her

eyes were shining, her face glowing. "You look like you could go another eight hours," he said.

"I'm wiped out, but it's a good kind of tired."

He tilted his head and gave her a wry look. "You sure you feel okay? Had a bit of the bubbly, did you?"

His gibe didn't dent her mood one bit. She was as bright as her name, and he found himself completely enchanted.

Danger, danger, Nick D'Angelo.

"It's just I've never witnessed a big Italian wedding before. It's so emotional and...loud."

"What other way would a wedding be? It's a celebration."

She shook her head. "In my neck of the woods, weddings are formal affairs where it's all about having the best guest list and all the right people associated with the planning." She did that eyebrow thing and raised a pretend cigarette holder to her mouth. "You know, this was far better than Muffy and Vernon's wedding last year, darling. How clever of them to have rented the entire Sears Tower for this little affair. Is that The Donald I see over there?" She dropped her hand and the upper crust accent and added, "The weddings I've been to have had all the excitement of a corporate merger." She laughed. "Which, come to think of it, most of them are."

"Don't kid yourself," he said. "All those same things are going on here, just with an old-world accent. Tradition and heritage are big things in my world, as well. Bringing these two families together has probably been as tricky as the Time-Warner merger."

Sunny's attention wandered to the bride as she danced by on the arm of her glisteny-eyed father. "Well, all I can say is you know how to have a good time while doing business."

Nick followed her gaze. It was the weirdest thing, but he had this sudden vision of what it would be like to whirl around the dance floor with his own daughter on his arm on her wedding day. The panic that should have immediately followed such a thought didn't rise and choke him like it would have a few weeks ago.

"Her father's only teary-eyed because he knows he hasn't gotten my bill yet."

Sunny rolled her eyes. "You can make this all about work if you want, but leave me my fantasies, okay?"

He grinned and moved closer to her, and his mouth was by her ear before he knew it. "And just what fantasies do you have, Sunny?"

SUDDENLY THEY WERE standing far too close to one another, and the room seemed stiflingly hot. *I shouldn't have provoked him.* Sunny tried to shift her attention to the dance floor, but somehow he filled her entire line of vision. Any hope the question was rhetorical died when she looked into his questioning eyes.

She shrugged. "Nothing specific. Just that I was never that little girl who grew up dreaming of her wedding day, planning out every little detail in my head. But..." Her gaze drifted from his, even if she only saw the dancers in her mind's eye. "But today there was so much.... Well, this sounds silly and trite. But there is so much love here in this room. Between the bride and groom, of course, but also between their families and for their families." She looked into his eyes. "Warmth and love in such abundance. Maybe if I'd known it could be like this, I'd have been dreaming about it, too."

He brought his finger to her chin, and Sunny felt a shuddering sensation shoot through her at his touch. It was gentle and brief, just a stroke along her jaw before he moved his hand away.

"I thought all princesses had fairy-tale lives with fairy-tale princes and Cinderella weddings."

"Maybe my life isn't the fairy tale you want to think it is."

"I was just coming to that very same conclusion." He shifted the tiniest bit closer. "Maybe if you told me more about it, I'd have a better understanding."

"Why? What could interest you about my life?"

His fingers lingered once again on her cheek. A strand of hair had come loose from her bun, and he tucked it behind her ear. "Maybe it's not your world but you I want to understand more."

Sunny couldn't move, could barely breathe. She'd

known the man had charisma, but this kind of focused intensity was mesmerizing.

"Why?" she asked, not caring that she sounded ridiculously breathless. Right here, right now, standing in this room with gowned and tuxedoed people dancing around them, it seemed perfectly right to be staring into the eyes of a gorgeous man and feeling a bit light-headed. "I'm only an employee."

Nick grinned, and she felt her knees dip. "You've never been only an employee. You have corporate CEO written all over you. Along with country-club matron and society doyenne."

Talk about having your balloon popped. She stepped away, the whirling room instantly coming into sharp and disappointing focus. It had been stupid to let herself get swept away.

"Right now the only thing I am is kitchen help at D'Angelos restaurant." She unbuttoned her white jacket and peeled it off. "I came here to get away from people who assume I have to be something because I'm supposed to be, or because I was born to be. I can't help it that I was born and raised a Chandler. But it's not like I expect anything because of it. You say you want to know the real me, and yet you already have me pigeonholed, too." She shoved the jacket into his hands. "I quit."

"Sunny, wait!"

She kept right on walking, picking up speed as she

went, not stopping until she was in the alley behind the kitchen of the rented hall.

She stood there and took a deep gulp of air. Well, that probably hadn't been her brightest move to date, but she'd apparently found her last straw.

Nick burst through the back door and came to a skidding halt in front of her. "Sunny, take this." He held out the jacket.

She folded her arms. "What part of 'I quit' didn't you understand?"

"I didn't mean to insult you back there. I was making an observation, sort of stating the obvious."

Heat flared inside her again. "Which is what?"

He raked his hand through his hair. "Come on, even you have to admit that you don't exactly fit the mold of a typical D'Angelos kitchen helper."

All her righteous indignation suddenly fled, and exhaustion and defeat filled her instead. "Apparently I don't fit any mold." She turned to leave. To go where, she had no idea, but she couldn't stay here a moment longer.

"I'm sorry."

He'd said those words to her before, but something in his quiet tone made her stop.

"What is it you're trying to prove, Sunny?"

She turned. "Nothing. That's just it. Can't I just show up and work? I've done nothing but give my best effort for you. I only asked to be accepted for the person I am, the one who shows up and does the job."

"I respect your work. I know it wasn't easy tackling something you had no training for. And I wasn't aiming to insult you. You talked about your world, and I was merely stating that, despite your hard work for me, I look at you and I don't see you as a kitchen worker."

"Why? It's good enough for you. So why isn't it good enough for me? If I show up and do the work, than why can't I just look like what I am?"

He dared to step closer, holding her gaze in an almost challenging way. She didn't retreat. No more retreating, she knew that now.

"Because you don't," he said quietly. "You could work in my kitchen for the next fifty years and I will look into your blue eyes and your beautifully refined face and at the delightfully graceful way you carry yourself and listen to your perfect diction and picture you in drawing rooms taking afternoon tea."

"That's breeding, upbringing. I can't help how I look or how I talk. I'm hardly a snob."

"No, I never said that or meant it. But you said yourself you don't fit in, so you do see what I'm getting at."

"All right. But it's not because of my background." She searched for the right words to explain. "It's because... I've discovered that working in a restaurant, or even running one, isn't going to be my particular passion. It is yours, so it suits you. If it *were* mine, then it should suit me, too, no matter whose blood runs through my veins. It's not about blood or breeding, it's about what's in here." She pressed her fist to her heart. "You'd be surprised to hear this, but you and my grandfather have a lot in common. He spends all his time telling me who I am and who I will be, as if my heritage predetermines every thought or feeling I will ever have. You look at me and see my genes and hear my education in my voice and expect me to be that person, too. Neither of you has ever bothered to figure out who I really am."

"Who are you, then?"

She flung her hands in the air, no longer angry at him, but the confusion and frustration she'd been dealing with for weeks all bubbled over. "I don't know! How in the hell am I supposed to figure out who the hell I am if no one will just let me be myself long enough to figure it the hell out?"

He smiled, and it was all she could do not to sock him. She began to understand his sisters' appetite for physical violence.

"What," she demanded heatedly, "is so amusing?"

"You. I've never heard you swear like that. I always thought it would be fun to make you lose that incredible cool of yours."

"Fun?"

"Well, I wasn't thinking of making you lose it in anger."

That stopped her.

He moved closer still, and his smile faded. "Do you really care that much?"

That took her off guard. "What do you mean?"

"Do you really care what we think of you? Me, or your grandfather, or anyone? Why does it matter?"

She opened her mouth to defend her point of view, but she couldn't. It was a good question. Dammit. "I love my grandfather, despite how frustratingly closed-minded he can be. I suppose I'd like to think he loved me enough to allow me to find what makes me happy and pursue it. Even if it's not related to the Chandler empire."

"Fair enough." He put his hands on her shoulders and drew her closer. "So what about me? Why does my opinion matter?"

His touch rattled what little she had left of her composure, but she made no move to break contact. She tried to look away, but his gaze demanded she return it. His expression demanded honesty. So she gave it to him. "I honestly don't know. Except it does. I admire what you do and how well you do it. I admire that and envy it, as well. One thing I have found here that I don't want to lose is the warmth and connection you all have. It's a big part of who you are. And I like who you are. I suppose I'd simply like for you, in turn, to respect me. To like me for who I am." A small smile twitched at the corners of her mouth. "Whoever the hell that might be."

At the gleam in his eyes, she felt her heart shift just

slightly off balance. "Maybe," she added, "it's because you do know who you are and enjoy what you do so much that I realize how much I want to find that for myself. And if you could look at me and see the real me, then maybe you could help me figure out just who the real me is."

"Maybe instead of defining who you are by how others perceive you, you should worry about making your own self happy and satisfied first," he said quietly. "The rest will follow. Or it will from those who are important to you. The others don't matter."

"I'm trying, Nick. It's a lot harder than I thought it would be."

"Maybe you're looking for big changes all at once. Maybe you should focus on the little things, one step at a time. You'll get there."

"Maybe. I hope so."

"Let me ask you one thing." He pulled her closer, his hands still on her shoulders. "Do you really want to leave the restaurant?"

"I don't know. But I don't want to leave the apartment or the neighborhood. I like your family. I like it here."

"Okay. One step accomplished. Can I ask you a favor?"

"Depends."

"Could you stay until the end of the month? I'll be able to get a replacement more easily then. Of course, if you change your mind, you can stay indefinitely."

"I pass my probation then, huh?"

"I have a feeling that you could pass any test given to you, if you want to badly enough."

She grinned. "Thank you. That's possibly the best compliment I've ever received. I'll stay. It will give me time to decide what small step to take next."

"Can I give you a suggestion?"

"Which would be?"

"Would you enjoy kissing me? Would that be something Sunny Chandler, the woman standing in front of me right now, would like to do?"

She was still for a moment as his words sank in, then her entire body responded for her. "Yes."

"Thank God. I've been dying to taste that mouth of yours since the moment I met you." He lowered his head and ended that wait.

8

WHEN NICK lifted his head a long minute later, they were both breathless.

"I'm..." She paused to clear her throat. "I'm... That was some small step."

"Yeah." Nick couldn't be funny or cool about it. Sunny Chandler's mouth was like nothing he'd ever experienced in his life. "There isn't a chef in the world who could create something that tastes as fine as you."

She laughed.

His entire world had just been rocked, and she was laughing. But her eyes were shining, and he found himself laughing along with her. "Hey, it's not often I'm moved to poetry." Like never. He'd never been moved to say anything like that.

"It wasn't a bad line."

"Line? I don't do lines." She did that eyebrow thing, and he relented. "Okay, maybe when I was Joey's age, but I don't need lines to communicate my feelings to a woman."

Her eyes went a bit darker at that. Good.

"My apologies. I guess I just assumed—"

"Never assume anything with me, Sunny. Fair's fair, right? I'm trying to do the same with you."

She dipped her chin. "Yes."

He touched her face, urging her gaze to his. "I meant what I said. Your mouth is...a delicacy."

To his delight, she blushed. He stroked her cheek. "Not that I'm assuming anything," he said, getting a smile out of her, "but I can't be the first to say such things."

"Then you would be surprised." Her smile faded. "I really... You...you really... Your kiss..." She broke off with a laugh. "Apparently your kiss has the opposite effect on me. I'm tongue-tied."

He smiled and bent his head. "Here, let me untangle it." She tasted every bit as sensational the second time. Even when he thought he knew what to expect, she was the unexpected. His voice was rough when he finally spoke. "Like a seven-course meal, only I'm not getting nearly full enough."

Her cheeks bloomed again. With her lips red and wet from his mouth, it was all he could do not to sweep her up and take her to the nearest bed. His.

"You're..." Again, she had to clear her throat. "Poetry suits you," she said softly. "I wouldn't have expected you to be so sweet."

He hoped he looked properly horrified. "Sweet? I wasn't aiming for sweet." Actually, he hadn't been aiming for anything. This was no longer about getting her out of his system and out of his life. He had no idea what it *was* about, not yet, anyway, but he'd spoken directly from his heart. "Sexy and endearing, maybe."

"It was very endearing. In fact, I could get used to being compared to food."

"Cuisine." He ran his fingertip along her bottom lip, immensely gratified when he felt her shudder at his touch. "Food is too generic a word for you." She moved from his touch, but he didn't let her look away. "I know I'm supposed to be unassuming about you, but when I look at you, Sunny, I see fine things. And the taste of your mouth only confirms it."

Instead of getting her back up again, his comment brought on a smile that could only be termed devilish. Unexpected. Yes, she was certainly that. He couldn't wait to find out what she'd do next. And next. And next.

"Well, fair is fair," she said. "When I look at you, I see...hot things."

He didn't think his body could be any harder. He'd been wrong. "Hot?" he said hoarsely. He crowded closer to her, bumping her body with his. "Hot how?"

Her composure slipped when their bodies connected. "Earthy hot, passionate hot." She swallowed hard when he grinned. "You're a very passionate man. About your family, your work."

He pulled her into his arms. "Then it should follow I'd be passionate about...everything. Right?"

"Right," she said faintly, just before he kissed her again. "Dear God," she said, then swore under her breath when he finally left her lips to trail kisses toward her ear.

"I find I enjoy making you swear, Sunny Chandler."

"What...what do we do now?" she murmured against his throat as he tucked her against his chest.

It was either hold her tight or take her right there in the alley. The wall behind her was looking real good. "I don't know about you, but I'm not nearly through feasting yet."

She smiled at him. "You know what? Neither am I."

That was all it took. That simple admission, and he was over-the-edge gone. "You communicate your feelings pretty well yourself," he said tightly, trying to get himself under control. He still had a business to run here. Dammit. "Let me go talk with the Costanzas and turn things over to Louis." She started to pull away a little, but he held on tightly, gratified when she let him.

"And then?" she asked.

And then I want to take you to my bed and feast upon you until we're both fully sated. It was what he wanted to say. More flowery words. They came into his mind, all but formed on his lips. She did that to him. And he discovered he liked it.

"Then we go spend time together," he said. "So I can discover the real Sunny, and you can discover whatever you want to know about me. Your choice where."

He could see the dreamy pleasure start to fade from her mind as reality fought its way in. No, no, he didn't want reality. And he wanted her to forget, too, if just for a little while. It would all come crashing back too soon, anyway. His world, her world...and the chasm between the two.

Without warning, he kissed her as deeply as he knew how, pouring all his hungry passion into the kiss. When they were like this, there was no chasm between them. In fact, there had never been anything that felt so close, so predestined, as this.

When he let her go, she stumbled, and her eyes were dark and stormy. He felt much better. Passion brewed inside his Sunny.

"My ride is there. Here's the keys. I'll be right back." He pressed the keys into her hands, smiling into her dazed face, and left before rational sense returned to either of them.

He went into the dark hallway at the back of the rented hall, wondering what in the hell he was doing with her. "Finding out," he said under his breath. He had to find out what it was about her that wouldn't let him go.

He hoped it took a good long time.

SUNNY WALKED in a sort of trance to Nick's vehicle and unlocked it. It wasn't until she was sitting in the front seat that she realized this was not the sedate businessman's sedan he'd driven her to Father Sartori's in. So he had two cars...though she'd have guessed sports car, typical toy for a successful young bachelor. But a four-wheel drive truck? It wouldn't have been her tenth guess. And from the looks of it, he'd managed to find a place to do some off-road playing. Funny, he'd never struck her as the type to play.

Apparently she'd been doing as much conclusion-jumping about him as she'd accused him of doing about her. Only he'd been a lot more graceful in pointing it out to her than she'd been. And now that she thought about it, she really couldn't fault him. Like her, he'd only been working with the facts he had in front of him. It wasn't as if he'd used his conclusions against her.

Against her. She groaned under her breath as she recalled just how intensely wonderful it had been to be held against *him*.

Despite all her feverish dreams, she still couldn't believe what they'd just done, that they'd really taken the step. She blew out a shaky breath, thinking about what would happen next.

Her hair net slid to her neck, and she gasped and yanked down the mirror as she tugged it off. "Oh, God," she groaned. She'd taken what felt like the most important step she'd ever taken with a man...looking like something from a horror show. All flushed and mussed up. Makeup gone and hair about as awful as it got.

He'd spouted poetry comparing her to gourmet cuisine when she looked like this?

She looked worse than drive-through fast food at the moment. Well, she'd wanted him to see the real her. "And it doesn't get any more real than this." She shook her head and snapped the mirror up.

Was he having second thoughts? she wondered. Was he right now wishing he'd never kissed her? It would change everything. Already had. Was she ready to go further?

"To fling, or not to fling," she murmured. "That is the question."

Nick came out of the rear entrance of the hall. He was still dressed in server attire. Black pants, white shirt, black bow tie and black jacket, befitting the occasion. The wind tossed his hair around his head, and the black jacket emphasized the sharp line of his jaw and his dark eyes. He looked up, spied her staring at him and smiled. A dazzling smile.

Fling, she thought, decision made. She might be confused, but she wasn't stupid.

Nick opened the driver door, slipped his jacket off and undid his tie, then put them both in the back before sliding into the front seat.

When he shut the door, the previously roomy interior seemed to shrink to cozy intimacy. Had she really been in this man's arms moments ago, getting the daylights kissed out of her?

Her fingers curled with the need to reach out and touch him. Did she have the right to touch him? Whenever, however, wherever she wanted? She didn't think he'd say no. *Well, Sunny, aren't you here to figure out what it is you want and go get it?*

She touched him.

She lifted her hand to his collar and smoothed it, then fingered the hair that brushed his collar. What she really wanted to do was grab him and pull him across the stick shift on top of her.

"What?" he asked, apparently seeing the indecision in her eyes. He took her hand from his nape, turned it palm up and pressed a very hot kiss to the center of it. Then, while she was still melting into a puddle, he lifted his gaze enough to capture hers and gently sank his oh-so-white teeth into the tender skin beneath her thumb.

If it was possible to climax from palm fondling, she would have, right then and there.

"Where to, milady?" he asked, still holding her hand.

She tried to speak, not that she had the faintest clue what she'd have said, but her throat had dried up.

"Outdoor recreation?" He flashed that grin again. "Or indoor?"

She swallowed hard. "I...indoor."

His eyes went incredibly dark, and he tugged her

hand so she leaned across the seat. He tucked his hand around her nape and pulled her the rest of the way, until she was almost sprawled into his lap. His kiss was hot and demanding.

Dear God, when she'd thought of him as a real man, she hadn't known the truth of it. Men of her acquaintance didn't have this kind of raw passion.

For the first time in her life, she wondered if she was enough. Raw enough to be able to satisfy him.

He must have sensed it, because he broke their kiss to say, "What? Do you want me to stop? Too fast? Too soon?"

She shook her head. "No." She looked at him, and he brushed her hair from her cheek. It was little gestures like that that melted her heart. "But..."

"But what? You're used to a more refined kind of courting?"

This time she didn't take offense. Because he was right. "Yes, but that's not it." She shifted nervously, and again he smoothed his hand over her hair and face reassuringly. "It's just that you're so open and honest about what you feel, and, well, I've spent my life learning to curb my feelings, my passion, channel it all in appropriate directions. You..." She smiled. "You make me want to be inappropriate."

"I have no problem with that."

She stroked his cheek. "What if it's not enough? If I'm not...enough?"

He laughed. "Trust me, Sunny. You're enough. So much in fact, I'm drowning in you."

His easy assurance thrilled her. But she said, "I'm not used to just letting it all go." She let out a self-deprecating laugh. "I guess what it comes down to is I've always had polite sex." There, she'd said it.

Nick laughed again, but there was affection in his tone. He pulled her mouth to his. "Well, we're about to change that." He looked into her eyes, his own smiling and confident and, most of all, wanting her. "Kiss me, Sunny. *You* kiss me. We'll just take it from there."

So she did. And realized that, with the right man, finding raw passion was not only possible, but wonderfully easy.

She framed his face, loving the slight bristle of his burgeoning five o'clock shadow. She loved the taste of him, too. His lips were full and warm and pliant. She felt his grip on her tighten as she dipped her tongue into his mouth, tentatively at first, then more deeply when she heard the moan in his throat. She felt it. Primal. That's how this felt. And it was only a kiss.

Her body tightened as thoughts of where this was going began to fill her mind. Carnal thoughts that she desperately wanted to turn into reality. Right now. "Take me home," she managed to say hoarsely.

He lifted his head enough to look into her eyes. "I'd

like to take you to my home." His voice was so rough, it all but vibrated her skin.

She nodded, understanding. Making love to her in his brother's bed would not be her first choice, either.

HOW THEY MANAGED to get to his condo without to-taling his truck or anyone else's was a mystery. She couldn't even remember most of the drive. He'd been doing amazing things to her knees with his fingertips, and she'd been tasting the side of his neck and dis-covering that his thighs were every bit as rock hard as she'd thought they might be.

She hardly noticed the building, other than that it was on a quiet side street. It felt like forever before he found his key for the lobby door. They raced each other up the stairs, and any awkwardness that might have happened at his door vanished when he leaned her against it and took her mouth in such a way that she was begging him to take her to bed. Or on the floor right here in the hallway. Whatever. She was out-of-her-head wild for him, wanting and needing as she'd never been in her life. It was exhilarating. Liberating.

He opened the door and they stumbled backward into his condo. She didn't even take time to notice his decorating style or lack of it. Her eyes were only on him. He closed the door and kissed her as she leaned against it. His shirt buttons opened slowly beneath her fumbling fingers, as hers did beneath his.

"Wait, wait," he said, as breathless as she was. "I'm not making love to you in my foyer." His grin surfaced, and she took a deep, steadying breath. For all the good it did. "Not this first time, anyway."

So much for getting steady.

"Do you want a drink or anything?"

She shook her head. "Just you. I just want you." She took immense pleasure in the instant reaction she got from him. He pulled her close, then swung her into his arms, eliciting a squeal of surprise. "Really, I can walk," she said.

"Really, I want to carry you. In fact, I just realized I've always wanted to do that."

And she discovered she'd always wanted it, too. Who knew? It was every bit as romantic as it always looked in the movies. "I'm no little thing," she cautioned.

He grinned and rested her hip against the cradle of his. "Neither am I."

He carried her through a living room that passed in a blur of tans and blues and down a short white hall into a bedroom that was all navy walls and heavy oak furniture. Her eyes closed blissfully as he kissed her again while they tumbled into his bed.

9

NICK WANTED all of her beneath all of him as soon as
possible. His hands trembled as he tugged her T-shirt
from the waistband of her slacks.

She was shaking, too. He paused and gazed into
her eyes. "Are you sure about this?"

She nodded, her eyes huge, her skin flushed and
her lips wet and puffy from his kisses.

"If...if I do anything you're not comfortable with,
you have to promise you'll tell me. Too fast, too hard,
too slow, whatever. Tell me. Promise?"

She reached up to stroke his face. He felt his heart
make a strange shift, as if settling deeper in his
chest...and swelling. God, everything was swelling.

"Promise," she said softly. She laid her fingers over
his. "Let me do that." She pulled her shirt up and off,
revealing a lacy white bra.

"Like unwrapping a gift." He stroked his thumb
over the silk covering one distended nipple, then the
other, enjoying the storm brewing in the depths of her
blue eyes. His body jerked in response to her gasp
and the light arch of her back. "You're so damn ex-
quisite," he said roughly. "And don't ever think your

body isn't honest or passionate enough. Look what it does for my touch." He rubbed his thumb over the silk again, this time eliciting a moan from her. He dipped deeply into her mouth with his tongue, immensely gratified when she moaned even louder.

He trailed his lips across her cheek and down her throat. "I want to taste you, Sunny. All of you." He opened the front clasp and let the flimsy material slide from her skin. She cried out when his mouth closed over her bared nipple, her fingers sinking into his hair. She was pulsing beneath him, and his body ached to feel the curves and length of her beneath him. But he resisted, possibly the hardest thing he'd ever done.

He continued his delicious journey of discovery as he undid her black work trousers and slowly slid them down her thighs until she could kick them off. "Matching white silk panties." He grinned at her. "How appropriate of you."

She smiled, then stunned him by pulling him on top of her. "I don't want to be appropriate."

"Good." He ground the word out.

She pushed at his shirt until he shook it off, then tugged his T-shirt from the waistband of his pants, but as he went to help her, she covered his hands. Her wicked smile gave him goose bumps. Intensely pleasurable goose bumps.

"My turn to undress you."

"By all means," he said, choking lightly on the last word as her hands slid beneath his T-shirt.

She stroked his nipples just as he'd stroked hers. His hips moved off the bed of their own volition. Dear God, that felt insanely good. "I don't think.... No one has ever..." Whatever else he'd been about to say was lost in a long, deep growl of satisfaction as she yanked his T-shirt up enough to taste his nipples with her mouth. "Oh..."

"Is something wrong?"

"Only you stopping that would be wrong. Sweet Jesus, don't ever stop doing that."

He felt her grin against his skin. That did it. He yanked his T-shirt the rest of the way off. His pants were gone a second later.

She stopped him with a hand to his briefs. "Can I?"

He had instant visions of her mouth doing the same sort of discovery routine it had just performed under his T-shirt. He nodded weakly. "Oh, yeah."

She whispered in his ear. "Now, you have to promise me you'll tell me if I'm going too fast, too hard...or too slow."

He could only nod.

She took her own sweet, excruciating time traveling south. By the time her fingers...and her tongue...reached his elastic waistband, he was about one second away from total loss of control. He wove his fingers through her hair and urged her up to his mouth. He kissed her hard and long, a venting of every need and want he had, too many even to count.

"Why did you stop me?" she murmured.

"One more second and we'd have been done before we began."

"Next time?"

He thought his eyes might have rolled back in his head for a moment. Lord, what had he done to deserve her? "Did I mention I am enjoying your search to find yourself quite immensely?" he said.

She cupped him through his briefs, making his hips jerk. "Immensely is right."

He tugged off his briefs, glorying in the sudden chill of the air against his heated flesh. It gave him the slightest of edges, a fraction of control. He slipped a finger beneath the thin strap holding her panties on her hips. "How attached are you to these?"

She looked both amused and amazed. "Not very."

"Good." With one tug, the strap was history. He slid her on top of him so she straddled him. Words were lost to them both when she settled over him. So hot and wet, he felt the surge coming over him again, rushing him right to the brink. He lifted her hips and was pressed against her when some semblance of reason came over him. "Protection." He barely managed to grind the word out.

"Pill," she gasped.

"Thank God." He pulled her down on him, and their joint groans filled the room as he filled her. She pressed down on top of him, her knees clamped to his thighs.

He wasn't going to last long, not this time, possibly not the next dozen times. He shifted and tucked her beneath him, then sank all the way inside her. She lifted her hips, moving with him instantly, easily. Unbelievably, the pleasurable tension wound even tighter. He felt the rush overtake him. His head was back, eyes squeezed shut as he began to give himself over to it.

But something wasn't right. He felt alone all of a sudden, and it felt wrong, simply wrong. He managed to open his eyes, look into her face. And when her gaze met his and he saw what was in her eyes...then he came. Hard, almost crushing pleasure drove through him...and he never stopped gazing deeply into her beautiful eyes. He fell into them, as what he saw there was even more intense than the other sensations rocketing through him combined. It wasn't just coming, the release itself, it was coming inside of her, and seeing the pleasure in her face. In every movement of her body.

She held him against her, bearing all his weight even when he tried to shift off her.

"Not yet," she whispered. "Not yet."

He was more than happy to comply. His head was reeling. What had just happened?

She was stroking his hair, his back. Then he felt warm, little kisses being pressed against his neck.

And it was the most natural thing in the world to turn his head and take her mouth. Softly this time, almost reverently.

It shocked him to realize that this time, these moments, right now, were crucial in some way he couldn't fully comprehend.

He turned to his side and curled her into him, twining his legs with hers. He pushed the hair from her face. "We're not through yet." He didn't know why, but he had to make sure she knew that. She couldn't leave him yet. Maybe not ever. Not until he figured out what had happened to him.

She smiled. "Okay."

A sort of lassitude stole through him, and his feelings of apprehension diminished. She was here, she was his, for now. His grin came easily. "*You're* not through yet."

Her smile faltered. "Oh? And what am I not through with?"

"Discovering. Neither am I."

"What do you have left to discover?"

Millions of things. Her every thought, idea and opinion, every last detail of her held enormous appeal. But right at this specific moment... "I want to discover what it feels like to make you come apart with the same intensity I just felt."

Her eyes widened slightly, then went dark again. He saw, almost felt her swallow hard. "Well. Okay." His heart slipped a notch. "I wasn't complaining, but I suppose fair's fair and all."

Nothing was fair. If life was fair, this dream would never end. He would deal with reality later, maybe in another life.

"Fair's fair," he agreed. And with a smile, he slowly worked his way down her body with his mouth and hands until she was sheened with sweat and writhing beneath him, and to his shock, he was ready for her all over again.

There was no poetry profound enough to describe the taste of her on his tongue. She was sweet perfection. It should have been more awkward, this first time, learning her body, and yet he brought her to the brink almost effortlessly, simply taking his pleasure and all but drowning in the knowledge that it was her pleasure, too. When she went over the edge, his hips dug hard into the mattress of their own volition, the joy he felt in pleasing her almost as strong as the climax he'd experienced. He'd always thought himself a generous lover who took care of his partner, but this was on a different plane altogether.

He moved up her body. And when he locked his gaze on hers and sank fully into her again, the shattering emotions that rocketed through him when he realized the hot, slick wetness coating him was from both of them could not be denied. There was no explanation. The power of their union defied description.

He gathered her into his arms and held her. He wanted to tell her, wanted to make sure she knew that this had been no ordinary event for him. So far from it, it should have terrified him. Only it didn't. A smile spread across his face as he allowed the joy of this moment to wash over him.

She snuggled more deeply into his arms, and he felt her smile against his chest. "You would have done well a few hundred years ago."

He kissed the top of her head. "Meaning?"

She propped her chin on his chest and looked into his eyes. "Well, let's just say, as explorers go, Lewis and Clark got nothing on you."

He laughed and kissed the tip of her nose, then dropped another more lingering kiss on her mouth. Her eyes were all dark and dreamy again. He loved that. That his kisses did that. Contentment like he'd never known seeped into his veins. "I could spend every Saturday like this."

"Whoa," she teased. "Pretty hearty praise from a workaholic."

"I'm not a workaholic. I know how to have a good time."

"Boy, do you ever!"

He grinned, but persisted. "I am not all work and no play."

"You do put in long hours, you're in your office till the wee hours, and I've never known you to take a day off in the three weeks I've been here."

"I take time off, just maybe not whole days at a time. I'm taking time right now, as an example."

She sighed lustily. "For which I will forever be indebted to Louis." She stroked her palm over his chest. "I know you enjoy your work, that it's your life."

"A life I like very much."

"It's obvious that it gives you as much as you give it, which is a great deal."

He covered her fingers. "It's not just dedication or an overdeveloped work ethic, though Lord knows Bennie and Sal drummed that into all of us from a young age. I'm not doing it for the success or because it's family tradition."

"Did you ever feel that pressure? To carry on the family business?"

"I guess, but it wasn't really a problem, because I wanted to do it. I grew up in the restaurant and can't imagine being anywhere else."

"Had you wanted to do something else, what would your family have said?"

"There would have been disappointment, but I think they would have supported me if they knew it was what I really wanted, like we all support Joey in his career choice." He laced his hand through hers and drew her fingers to his lips, kissing each one, un til he had her full attention. "I'm sorry your family isn't close like mine."

"You're lucky to have that kind of support. To know it's just there for you."

"Absolutely. I honestly can't imagine what would have happened to me when my parents died if I hadn't had Joey and even my sisters—though I'll deny that to my grave."

She smiled, but there was a sadness in her eyes that tugged at him. "I know it must have been hard for my grandparents to have to deal with the death of their only son and take on the care and responsibility of me. They never once complained, and I never once felt I was a burden to them. Far from it. I was everything to them, and they made sure I knew it."

"Maybe you had too much focus, too much love."

"Is there such a thing as too much love? I thought so, until I met your family. The abundance of love here is overwhelming."

"No, that was the abundance of noise overwhelming you," he teased, earning a small smile.

"It does take getting used to, the noise and constant activity. But I like it. And there is such affection, even in the arguing. It's not at all stifling, your family's love, it just absorbs you. I'm very grateful for the way they've taken me under their wing. It's given me a lot to think about."

"Maybe your grandparents placed all the hopes and aspirations they'd had for their son on you."

"Absolutely. My dad apparently thrived in the Chandler business. I was too young when they died to remember much, but it was always assumed I'd have the same enthusiasm."

"But you didn't."

She shook her head. "I felt like such a traitor for even thinking about not taking on the full mantle of responsibility that comes with being born a Chandler. Like I wasn't supposed to fulfill only their expectations, but those of my parents, as well. I honestly spent years thinking there was something really wrong with me, that I was just being selfish to not want what they had to give me."

"That's a pretty heavy burden for a child or even an adult."

"That's just it, they never saw it as a burden. Being a Chandler is a privilege to be cherished, because they both do. Honestly so. Chandler Enterprises, living that life is everything to them. They thrive on it, just like you do with yours."

Nick smiled. "So you're the black sheep, the renegade. Even the best of families have them. We have Joey."

She smiled at that, and he was glad to know he could lift the confusion and pain from her eyes, even momentarily.

"It's not wrong to want to have the freedom of making your own decisions," he said. "When you're told to love something, it doesn't mean you will. Or even that you should."

"I know. But I spent so many years trying to figure out what was wrong with me, doing what they wanted, hoping things would change for me, that I never figured out what it was I did want. It took me years to find the courage and confidence to not only believe it was okay, but to actually do something about it."

"What did it? What gave you the courage to leave?"

Her expression faltered, and he saw something in her eyes that sent a cold chill up his spine. "What, what is it?" He turned her face to his. "Honesty, Sunny. That is the one thing we started with, and I want it to stay that way. You can tell me anything."

"I went to grad school, doubled up my course load and got my master's in business communications. It was finally time for me to take my place with Grandfather. Only I just couldn't do it. I don't know, something finally snapped inside me. I had to have some time. I knew that the moment I walked in and saw the door with my name on it, my identity as a Chandler, first, last and always, was sealed forever. So I asked for some time."

The chill fingered its way from his spine to his heart. "*Some* time?"

She sighed softly, then looked into his eyes. "Six months. I wanted to figure out who I was before I became what I was expected to be."

"So, you're still planning on going back?" His heart squeezed painfully. Later. There would be time later to figure it all out. He pushed thoughts of the future away. And yet his heart seemed to pause while waiting for her answer.

"Yes. I have to."

hand on the shoulder, "but I really don't mean to talk about this much now. I just want to enjoy you and not ruin the afternoon Nick."

"Sunny."

"We aren't going back there anyway."

10

"WHY DO YOU have to?"

Sunny looked into Nick's eyes, not believing all she saw there. What did he expect from her? Had this meant something more to him than just a spectacular way to spend the afternoon? Could she let herself believe it might? Where would that leave her?

"I can't explain it," she said softly. She wished they'd never started down this conversational path. She wanted to enjoy her time with him. She'd have to deal with the future soon enough.

"Do you think you owe it to them?" he asked. "Or have you decided working with your grandfather is what you really want to do?"

She turned to shift away from him, but his arm came around her back and he cupped her face so she looked at him.

"You don't have to do anything you don't want to," he said intently.

"I know. I want bigger boundaries than they have. Fewer rules. I don't want to focus my entire life on being a Chandler and the family business. But—" She stopped, then impulsively reached up and kissed him hard on the mouth. "But I really don't want to talk about this right now. I just want to enjoy you and not make big life decisions this afternoon."

"Evening."

She glanced toward the window and realized that the summer sun had indeed begun to set. "I suppose you should be getting back to the store, so to speak. I can't remember the last time I was so...irresponsible." She started to move off him, but that iron band of an arm was still wrapped around her waist, pinning her to him. She didn't mind it a bit.

"We were not irresponsible. The reception was almost over, and I'm confident Louis took care of things. If not, I'd have heard from him by now. I already had the staff lined up at the restaurant for tonight."

For the first time, it occurred to Sunny what everyone must be thinking. The two of them had run from the reception straight to Nick's bed. The whole staff must be buzzing. Then another thought occurred to her. Two of Nick's sisters had been working the event today! She really must have been in a total hormonal fog to have not considered those consequences to their actions.

Nick grinned at her. "You didn't think this would remain a secret, did you?"

Sunny pushed at him, but Nick rolled her to her back, loosely pinning one wrist to the bed. The other was trapped between their bodies. "No running," he said, his tone teasing but his eyes very serious.

"I wasn't." But she wasn't so sure that was the truth. She'd needed to put what she'd done in perspective. "Won't this make things hard for you, too? Your family has made no secret they've been wanting to see us get together. I don't want to hurt them by misleading them or...or anything."

He took one hand to his mouth and kissed a very sensitive spot on the inside of her wrist. How did he know just the right spots to touch? *She* didn't even know she had those spots.

"Let me worry about my family." He trailed a series of light kisses along the inside of her wrist. "Right now, I'm where I want to be. Everything else will take care of itself." He slid on top of her. "Right now I just want to take care of you."

"I'm perfectly fine." More than fine—blissful, she thought. His body was warm, and amazingly she felt him stir against her yet again. Her hips were already shifting beneath his as she said, "You know, there is something about this work ethic of yours to be admired."

He grinned as he began to push against her. "I do like to be...on top of things."

"Oh, yes," she said, hissing the last word as he moved inside her. All thoughts of what would happen when they left this bedroom were blown from her mind on a flash of pleasure so bright, she couldn't concentrate on anything else. "Dear God, yes."

SUNNY SNUGGLED more deeply into her pillow and let her eyelids slit open to check the time. A second later, she shot up in her bed. Only it wasn't her bed. And it wasn't evening any longer. Or even night. That was sun shining in the bedroom window.

A warm hand wrapped around her arm. "Come back here."

Oh, God. After he'd made love to her that last time, she'd drifted off, thinking she'd rest a minute or two, then insist he take her home and check in on things at the restaurant. That had been—she shoved her hair from her face and squinted at the beside clock—nine hours ago.

"What's wrong?" Nick gently strolled her arm until she turned.

Just looking at him took her breath away. All dark and tawny, sprawled on white cotton sheets. There should be a law against looking so sinful and downright inviting. Her body was already gearing up to accept that invitation, too.

"I have to go," she said.

"There you go, *having* to do something again. Might I ask why?"

"Well, for one thing, shouldn't you be at the restaurant right now?"

His smile stayed in place, but his eyes turned a

shade less amused. "I'm a big boy, I know how to run my business. It's early yet. Why don't you tell me what's really wrong?"

"I—" She hesitated, then just spit it out. "I spent the night."

"And this is a problem—why?"

"Because I don't spend the night."

He looked at her for several long moments, then said, "Who made this rule? You? Or the Chandler empire?"

She wiggled her arm free, waiting for all the righteous indignation to fill her and give her the strength to leave his bed. Only it didn't come. And she didn't leave. Nor did she want to, if she were being honest.

And wasn't that what this whole thing was about? Being honest with herself?

"It was my rule, but I suppose it's grounded in Chandler expectations."

"And what expectations are those?" Nick propped himself up on his pillow. Her mouth went dry and she made herself look away from where the sheet draped dangerously low on his hips. Hips that could move so sinuously—

"Spending the night leads to speculation," she said quickly. "On the part of the person you spend it with."

"The kind of speculation that making love with that same person, performing such an intimate act with him, doesn't lead to?"

She felt her face burn, but continued. "I think you of all people would acknowledge that sex can be recreational while not automatically emotionally bonding or relationship-forming."

He smiled, obviously amused by her tone. "I guess I have a hard time seeing the Chandlers as people who encourage a lot of recreational sex."

Sunny surprised both of them by laughing. "Okay, so maybe I am a renegade. A little. And no, my grandfather didn't encourage me to sleep around. In fact, I don't sleep around. But, as you know, I wasn't a virgin, either. The men I dated, or was encouraged to date, were always appropriate and potential Chandler material."

"What? No black sheep on your dance card? You never strayed a bit?"

"At the risk of making you even more smug," she said dryly, "no, not until now."

His eyebrows lifted. "I'm hardly a black sheep."

She smiled. "Black enough. I tried very hard to please my grandparents because, after all, I felt I owed them everything. The least I could do was date men they would approve of. And, to be honest, it hardly seemed like a sacrifice."

His grin was downright wicked. "Do you still feel that way?"

She blushed. "I think I've maxed out your smug quotient for the day, so I'm going to politely decline answering that."

"Well, we all know how important it is for you to be polite."

He said it affectionately, and Sunny was pleased to discover that she didn't mind it. In fact, it was nice being able to be herself and yet laugh at herself, as well. "There's no use in pretending otherwise, so what can I say? I was always cautious and very certain to make it clear that there were to be no expectations beyond the moment."

"And the men in your life accepted that?" He laughed as if he couldn't imagine playing by those rules. And she couldn't see him doing so, either.

"You're right," he said, still chuckling. "You did have very polite sex."

Sunny could only shrug. "I never worried that any of them would pursue me if I didn't want to be pursued. I just made certain they didn't get the wrong idea in the first place. No sense in hurting anyone's feelings."

"No, we certainly wouldn't want anything messy and impolite like feelings involved."

She was offended. "I'm being pretty honest about my life here. It doesn't mean I don't have feelings or that I'd hurt anyone needlessly. If that kept things from getting messy, well then, I thought I was doing the right thing."

Nick didn't apologize. What he did was lean forward and run a finger down the side of her cheek, tucking a stray curl behind her ear. "So why are you in my bed now? Am I part of your renegade fling? Your chance to get a little messy before heading back to polite society? Only now it's morning and you realize I might see implications where none were intended? Do you regret straying from your polite little path?"

She shifted away from his touch but held his gaze directly. "Honesty, that's what you wanted from me, so here it is. Yes. In a way, you were my renegade fling."

He didn't register her words in any visible way. "And being here this morning is too messy for you?"

Trying to find the right way to explain, she paused. "It should be. That's why I automatically reacted the way I did."

There was a twitch in his jaw, a light tic at the vein in his temple. It was only then she realized how tightly he was holding himself in check. "But?"

"But there's nothing automatic about being with you. You're...different."

"Do you think I'm going to make problems for you now? Storm your world if you try to leave me?"

"Of course not!"

In a heartbeat she was flat on her back, the wind snatched from her lungs.

His face was inches from hers, his voice a low growl. "And what makes you so sure about that?"

There was no fear. She felt exhilaration, excitement and absolute anticipation. But not one shred of fear.

And that is what truly terrified her.

"When I go home, you will go on with your life as I go on with mine," she said breathlessly. "After all, wasn't it you who made it clear that you weren't in the market for marriage? I assume that also includes any kind of long-term commitment."

"What if I change my mind?"

She couldn't even contemplate that. She opened her mouth, but had no idea what to say.

He blew out a sigh. "Listen, never mind. If you ask me to leave you alone, I will. If you want to go home and don't want any further contact with me, then go."

"And if I don't want you to leave me alone...at least for now...then what?"

His eyes widened and her entire body responded. "Then I say stop worrying about the rules of polite society and go for what you want. You always do what you think is right for everyone else. Maybe it's time you were a little more selfish. If it gets messy, it gets messy. That's how the real world works." He leaned in, moving between her legs. "And if what you want is me, even for now, then by damn, take me, Sunny. We'll worry about the rest when it happens."

She didn't debate the invitation or analyze it for pros and cons and come up with a sensible reaction. She did what her gut and her heart told her to do. She shoved him over on his back and straddled him. "What if this is what I want?"

Nick's grin surfaced, sure and strong. "I absolutely encourage you to follow through on the decision."

The confidence and obvious affection in his eyes gave her an incredible sense of freedom. She could be whatever she wanted, whoever she wanted, with him. And he'd take exactly what was offered, nothing more...but also nothing less. He wanted the woman she was, and Sunny was realizing she liked the woman she was, too.

She leaned down and rocked her hips. "You know, for someone telling me to be selfish, you were pretty unselfish."

"Meaning?" he asked through gritted teeth.

"You could have let me make an ass of myself and walk out of here. Instead you made me face why I was reacting the way I was. And figure out what I want."

He grinned. "And who says that wasn't selfish on my part?" He grabbed her hips and swung her over him, making her groan deeply. "What if I knew all along I was what you really wanted?"

She collapsed on his chest, laughing and moaning at the same time. "Then I bow to your superior intellect and supreme insight."

He sat her upright and held her waist as he plunged into her. "Actually, one of the things I know for a fact about you is that, while you try to please everyone, you bow to no one. If you're with me—"

"Oh, I am..." She moved on him, smiling into his

face, relishing these moments perhaps more than any before.

"Then I know it's because I'm where you want to be."

He was right. She'd never had anyone really care enough to look beyond the name and the face and the stock holdings. It was a profound moment for her. He wouldn't be as easy as the men she'd dated. He'd make her look inside herself and examine her feelings and motives and decisions. He'd demand honesty.

And she found she wanted to give that to him. And to herself.

11

"SO, WHAT TIME is he picking you up?" Andrea reached over to tuck a stray curl beneath Sunny's hair net.

Sunny rolled her eyes. "He's not picking me up. We're working the festival together. It's not a date. Just like the wedding we worked wasn't a date."

Andrea's eyes sparkled. "Not at first, anyway." She raised her hands when Sunny gave her a mock glare. "I know. It's just fun to see you two near each other."

"Fun for whom?" Sunny said dryly.

Laughing, Andrea handed Sunny her apron. "Fun for anyone who can stand being that close to the flames."

Sunny merely shook her head and held her arms out while Andrea helped tie her apron. As Andrea fussed with the strings, Sunny realized how much her life had changed in the past four weeks. She had grown used to having one or two of Nick's sisters around, along with one or two cousins, half a dozen kids and all the noise and laughter that went with it.

The thought of being alone again, going back to

that cold, impersonal, oh-so-proper lifestyle made her stomach clench. Then Andrea was swinging her around and smiling while relating a fresh bit of gossip and, happily distracted, Sunny filed her worries away. Today was a workday, but it was also a fun day. She would have time to wander the street festival when her shift was up.

Wander the festival with Nick.

Two of Andrea's little ones ran screaming into the room, and Andrea efficiently steered them to the small living room. "Let me go bind these two in a chair. I'll be right back." The squeals reached a deafening pitch. "Bind *and* gag."

Sunny smiled, but her mind was still on Nick. Having his entire family underfoot had made her new relationship with him tricky. No matter how discreet she and Nick were, his family somehow gleaned every last detail. Nick laughed it all off. Sunny didn't find it that easy, but she was getting there. He might have been prepared, but Sunny had sorely underestimated their aptitude for pushing. And shoving. And downright dragging.

She had long since given up trying to make them understand that this relationship was merely a fun, noncommittal type thing. Operation Matrimony had kicked into high gear the instant the two of them left the wedding reception together. She tried not to think too much about what Nick would be left to deal with once she was gone. Mostly because she didn't want to think about leaving.

"So, your thirty days of probation are up as of today, huh?" Andrea came into the room and plopped on the bed.

Sunny craned her neck and looked past Andrea into the living room. "It's awfully quiet in there. Did you really gag them?" She was only partly kidding. She was in total awe of the D'Angelo sisters' ability to deal with so many kids. All at the same time.

Andrea smiled smugly. "Jell-O. It's basically the same thing."

"I didn't know I had any."

"You didn't. So I stocked some in your lettuce drawer a few days ago."

"Of course," Sunny said mildly. "Silly me, running low on Jell-O. What was I thinking?"

"I know." Andrea laughed. "I promise to come back with cleanser and ice picks to clean up the mess later."

Sunny didn't even blink. Another revelation of living with the D'Angelos. Mess happened. A lot. She'd learned to get way over the everything-in-its-place, white-glove-clean routine. Truthfully, that had been one of her easiest adjustments. Who knew being a slob was so much more fun?

"Mama Bennie says you're staying." Andrea eyed her closely.

Sunny realized answering this was tantamount to

shouting it from the rooftop. Everyone would know her decision inside the hour. But they'd find out soon enough. She'd already told Nick.

"I knew you wouldn't be able to walk away."

Sunny snorted. Snorted. A new noise for her, very unladylike. She liked it a lot. "Yeah, me and Carlo have a secret thing going." She clasped a hand dramatically to her chest. "I just couldn't leave him. He begged me to stay."

Andrea laughed. "Uh-huh. I knew that was the real reason. Nick will be shattered."

Sunny laughed, too, but went on. "Actually, I spent a long couple of nights trying to decide if I shouldn't leave D'Angelos and get a different job in the neighborhood."

Andrea looked both hurt and insulted.

Sunny hurried to explain. "It was because I didn't think it was appropriate to be having a relationship with the boss—no matter how casual," she felt compelled to add, for what good it would do. She continued over Andrea's objections. "I know, I know, but it was something I had to think about."

"Obviously Nick helped you to understand how ridiculous you were being. For goodness' sake, this is a family business. We all work with loved ones."

Sunny wisely didn't respond to that specifically. Love. It wasn't something she could even consider where Nick was concerned.

There was a loud shriek from the kitchen, and both

women dashed out of the bedroom, reaching the small dining area in time to watch Callie and Anthony finish smearing blue gelatinous goo all over the Formica table.

Andrea didn't even bat an eye. She cleaned their faces and hands in an efficient and downright miraculous fashion and scooted them down the stairs. "Go find Uncle Nicco. We'll be down in a minute."

Sunny crouched for the obligatory sticky-lipped kisses and thank-yous, smiling after them as they left. "You really are amazing with them, Andrea. I hope I'll be half the mom you are."

Andrea's eyes shot wide, and Sunny all but leaped to stop the assumption she saw dawning in her friend's eyes.

"No! Don't even think it. I was just dreaming in that vague someday kind of way. Don't you even start this on me, Andrea. Promise."

"Okay." But the gleam in her lovely dark eyes had Sunny swallowing a groan. "Have you always wanted kids?"

Sunny eyed her. She seemed sincere. Still, she wagged a finger. "I'm not having this conversation if it will bring that neonatal gleam back to your eyes."

Andrea's eyebrows lifted in a "who, me?" way that didn't fool Sunny for a second.

"I was just wondering," Andrea said, all innocence. "Are you expected to breed the next generation of Chandlers, being the last of the line, so to speak?"

"Oh, I'm sure that's in the grand plan. My grandmother is probably more interested in that aspect, being the sole arbiter of all things regarding the Chandler heritage. Grandfather's dreams are mostly centered around me running the business. I suppose the family and two-point-three children will be added in as a codicil or something at some point."

Andrea's smile fell. "I'm sorry, Sunny. I shouldn't have teased you about it."

"It's okay." She touched Andrea's arm. "Really. Actually, I never gave a great deal of thought to having my own kids. I've never really been around any."

"I'm surprised after being subjected to ours you haven't made the appointment to have your tubes tied already."

Sunny smacked at her arm. "Actually—and do not take this the wrong way—it's being around all of you that has made me think about it. I'm not sure what kind of mother I'd make. And I can't say as I'm thrilled with bringing kids into the world of Chandler Enterprises, et al." She shrugged, suddenly wishing she'd left this conversation alone.

"So, you aren't staying, then. Not permanently."

Sunny lifted her gaze and caught Andrea's solemn one. "That was never in the cards, you know that."

"Things can change, Sunny."

She took Andrea by the shoulders and pulled her

in close for a hug. "Your friendship has come to mean the world to me. And no matter what I do or where I go, I don't plan on losing it, okay?"

"Okay. But—"

"But there is a lot that I just can't explain."

Andrea opened her mouth as if to argue, then shut it again and nodded. "We won't spoil this day with talk about the future, okay?"

Immensely relieved, Sunny smiled and nodded. "Thank you."

But Andrea's charm surfaced quickly, and she winked as she sauntered to the front door. "Besides, life has a way of changing things when you least expect it to. Nothing is over till it's over."

"I give up," Sunny muttered, much to Andrea's delight.

As she followed her down the stairs, Sunny thought about the talk she and Nick had about why she'd stayed on. True to his word, he did know how to play. He'd taken her out for an afternoon of exhilarating off-road fun, which had led to other avenues of fun...and given her a whole new meaning for the phrase recreational vehicles. She smiled at the memory, then thought about the talk that had followed. It had lasted long into the night, and Nick had helped her make her decision to stay. His arguments had pretty much echoed Andrea's. She'd wanted to stay, to spend as much time with Nick as possible, for as long as possible. So, since no one else had a moral problem with her working for him, she wouldn't, either.

But Nick had been wonderful in respecting her request that they keep business time purely business. He'd made certain that they had plenty of nonbusiness playtime. Some of that time had even been spent outside his bedroom. And his truck.

Long lazy lunches, strolling through the various parks, walking the city streets. Nick knew an amazing amount of information about this city they'd both grown up in. She'd loved every second she spent with him.

She pressed a hand to her stomach to quell the butterflies that stirred there. Today was important. Even though Nick's family knew they were seeing each other, they'd never been openly together with his family. That would change today. Nick didn't seem at all concerned about the consequences of going public with their relationship in such a big way.

It seemed monumental to her. Everyone in the neighborhood would see them together. It would make leaving that much harder. And yet, she'd agreed with him that it was silly to try to hide the fact they were seeing each other. Neither had anything to hide or be ashamed about.

For now, she was right where she wanted to be, and that was what she was going to focus on—nothing else. She was happy. Truly, wonderfully happy. That was enough. More than she'd ever had before.

Andrea scooped up the purse she'd left in Nick's office and gave her hair one last pat in the tiny mirror on the back of the door. "I still say you should have invited your family today. It would be the best chance for them to meet everyone. And don't give me that look."

"What happened to let's not spoil today, hmm?"

As usual, Andrea ignored her, but her expression was laced with such affection Sunny couldn't be mad at her. Even when they annoyed her, she loved them. Maybe that was what family was really all about.

"You underestimate this neighborhood," Andrea said. "We'd treat your family with respect...and show them how to have a great time."

"Trust me, it's for the best this way." She'd tried, but there was no way to explain it to Andrea. Nick's family refused to believe that when push came to shove, every family wouldn't stand up for its own. Sunny knew better. The deafening silence from Haddon Hall this past month confirmed it. She'd have to deal with her grandparents at some point, but if they were content to let Carl continue his routine driving by as their sole means of communication, then so be it.

She felt a pang of sorrow. Nick's family was so close, it made it hard to acknowledge she couldn't turn to her own family for advice, or invite them to an event that meant something to her.

Andrea stopped her before they left the office. All

the teasing was gone from her rich, dark eyes. "I know you don't want me to talk about your future with Nick."

"Andrea—"

"I have to say this. I've never seen him like this with anyone, Sunny. I just wanted you to know that. This is serious for him."

Sunny shook her head. "It's only been a week, Andrea."

"A month. But time is meaningless in these things. Sometimes you just know."

Sunny refused to let herself think about that.

"I know you worry because he's been very vocal about commitment and his phobia to it, but he's the most dedicated—"

"It's not about commitment, Andrea, or a lack of one. It's…it's too complicated to explain right now."

"Well, I've given you plenty of chances to explain all these complicated things you know."

Sunny blew out a sigh. "I know. Maybe I just don't want to analyze it. We've decided to spend some time together. Why can't that be enough for now?"

Andrea laughed. "Because we're Italian and D'Angelos. There's no such thing as enough." She rubbed Sunny's arm. "But I promise to lighten up. At least for today." At Sunny's look, she smiled. "Okay, so I'll try to shut up for at least an hour. It's not in my nature to stand by and let people ruin their lives." She stepped into the hall, then looked over her shoulder. "Besides, you'll be too busy fending off the entire rest of the neighborhood. Give me a chance to step back and plot new strategies."

Sunny had to laugh. It was that or cry.

Andrea came back and grabbed her face, kissing first one cheek, then the other. "We love you, Sunny. You've already become like family to us. We just want to see you happy. Nick, too."

Sunny's heart warmed. "I know, Andrea," she said softly. "I know. You can't know how much all of you have come to mean to me."

Grinning, Andrea nodded, then held Sunny at arm's length. "Let's go feed some people, then tonight, we dance!"

Sunny was laughing as Andrea wandered to the front of the restaurant to track down her children, singing some Italian aria at the top of her lungs.

NICK WATCHED as Marina's kids grabbed Sunny and dragged her into another round of line dancing. It was almost midnight, and the revelry was still in high gear. He and Sunny had long since ended their shift working the food concession, but he'd hardly had a moment of time alone with her.

He should be frustrated, and a part of him was. He yearned to have her in his arms, with music filling the hot summer night air. But there was still time for that.

In the meantime, he had been very entertained just watching her enjoy her first street festival.

First street festival? Implying there would be others?

He veered away from that, and from wondering about the future at all. He'd found himself doing that an alarming number of times. Daily. He blamed it on his family and their incessant hounding over his new relationship with Sunny. He'd known it would be bad, but he hadn't counted on their pushing affecting him like this, making him think about what life would be like if Sunny stayed.

His eyes never strayed from her, not for a moment. Even as she wove in and out of the crowd, changing partners, laughing as she went. She had captivated him, of that there was no doubt. His family adored her. She adored them. It was clear in every look, every gesture.

He adored her. Or something very much like it.

Which meant what? She'd made it clear he was a fling, a wild and exciting adventure. But one that would end when Rapunzel had to return to her isolated tower. He was increasingly frustrated at the idea that she wouldn't consider not returning. Her grandparents hadn't made a single effort to contact her, as far as he knew. She'd decided to spread her wings, and they'd abandoned her. To him, this meant she'd done the right thing in trying to please herself first, then decide if she should please them. Or try. He had a feeling they weren't easily pleased, and that she'd give her life to the ordeal...and lose herself in the process.

She spun out of the dance and sat between two of his sisters, grabbing a cold beer. This was the real Sunny. The woman reveling in being out and alive in the world. He had to convince her this was where she belonged.

And if eventually they figured out that they also belonged together...well, that prospect was becoming less and less terrifying every day.

"Enough," he muttered, and stood. He made his way through the crowd until he was in front of her.

"You're too late," Rachel told him. "Her dance card was not only filled, it wilted and fell apart." She laughed, and everyone around her joined in. "Next time you need to be more on the ball."

Nick tried to smile, but there was this sense of urgency, and he didn't have time for banter. He needed to feel Sunny in his arms, needed to calm the whirl of emotions that had been swamping him all night. Shut it all out...and just concentrate on her.

He said a silent blessing when the band read his mind and shifted to a slow, bluesy song. He held out his hand. "Do you have one more dance in you?"

She nodded and rose, the smile on her face, and in her eyes a promise that sent his entire bloodstream on a sizzling ride.

His family and friends were immediately forgotten the moment she was in his arms. In fact, his world consisted of the slow rhythm pulsing around them...and the woman swaying to it.

"Sunny." It was all he managed to say before a groan of pleasure escaped him as she stepped closer to him. He wrapped her in his arms, and she rested her cheek on his shoulder. He pressed his lips to the soft spot beneath her ear. "I've been aching to have you like this all night."

"Why'd you wait?" she murmured.

"Because this will be the last dance for either of us tonight." He held her tightly against his hips, relishing the way she tightened her arms around his neck and kept her hips pressed to his. "I wanted you to enjoy the festival first. Because I knew the moment I got my hands on you, I wouldn't take them off again until you were hot and naked beneath me."

She groaned and kissed his neck. "Then we'd better dance our way to your car now, or I'm liable to embarrass myself in front of everyone you've ever known."

Grinning, Nick barely restrained himself from scooping her up in his arms and carting her off. He whispered that in her ear, and her eyes widened.

"You wouldn't."

"Oh, now you're all but daring me."

"I'm doing no such thing. I can walk to your car just fine."

"But think how much more romantic it would look if I swept you off your feet."

"Since when are you interested in being romantic?"

"Ouch?"

"You know what I mean. Romantic public displays. You know what your family would do."

He turned her face toward his. Her smile faded, but her eyes glistened. "I'm beginning to not really care about the pressure from my family. I'm feeling some pressure of my own."

"Yeah, I can feel that."

He groaned. "Yeah, well, that, too. But I wasn't referring to that."

Their dancing slowed almost to a stop as she stared into his eyes. "What are you saying, Nick?"

He stood there, under the lights, feeling the gaze of almost everyone in the crowd on him. None of it mattered. His whole world was in front of him, waiting for an answer.

A thousand thoughts poured through his mind. Did he tell her what was in his heart? Even if he wasn't all too sure yet how *he* felt about it? Should he wait? Come to terms with it first? Or should they figure it out together?

And what if she ran?

His hold tightened on her almost instinctively.

"Nick?"

"Not here. I need to be alone with you." And without thought, he did what he'd wanted to do all night. He scooped her up in his arms and carried her away.

The cheers of the crowd echoed in his ears, but he thought only of spending as much time as possible with the woman in his arms.

12

SUNNY WAS breathless by the time they reached
Nick's home. He hadn't spoken a word to her since
they'd left the festival.

She finally dared a glance at him as he drove into
his parking space. What was going on behind those
enigmatic dark eyes of his? The way he'd looked at
her while they were dancing. Shivers raced over her
skin, and there was an undeniable sense of anticipation infusing her.

What had she wanted him to say back there? What
did she want to hear from him now? Words of love?
Words of commitment? Either terrified her. She
wasn't ready. Not now. Maybe not ever. This was
supposed to be a fun fling, a walk on the wild side before going home.

Home.

She looked around her. The quiet neighborhood
street, the rows of family businesses all tucked away
snug for the night, the man who was taking her hand
and leading her toward...what? There was more than
another delicious night in his arms at stake here.

Part of her wanted to stop, demand he tell her what

was on his mind right now. Another part of her undeniably wanted to pull her hand free and run like hell. Run from having to make decisions that were very likely going to hurt someone somewhere. Why did she have to do that? She didn't want to have to choose.

Nick took her into his arms at his door and kissed her. "Sunny," he said roughly.

She pressed her finger to his lips. "Shh. Let's go inside, Nick." She looked directly into his eyes, afraid but secretly thrilled at what she found there. "Make love to me, Nick," she whispered.

The next several minutes were a blur of kisses and clothes being discarded through every room as they made their way almost frantically to his bed.

She tumbled him onto his back and straddled him. His eyes lit up in delight, and he held her hips.

"All that dancing has made your hips so..." He groaned as she writhed over him. "Flexible. Damn."

His back arched, and so did hers. It was always like this. Shockingly erotic and so damn pleasurable. Like she could drown in it...willingly.

He grinned at her as she set the pace. "Remind me to take you dancing more often."

She laughed, then moaned as the movement caused her to tighten around him when he slipped even more deeply within her. It was always like this, too. Teasing and affectionate and...fun. Wildly, amazingly fun.

She held onto his shoulders, and her hair cascaded forward to brush his face and chest.

His eyes closed as he delighted in the feel of her hair on him, something she knew he loved because he'd told her so. Many times. She enjoyed pleasing him. Each time they were together, she learned a little more about him and what to do to heighten their pleasure together. He had done the same and knew her body like no one else ever had. She couldn't imagine their lovemaking as anything other than a generous sharing of themselves where each put the pleasure of the other first.

Nick made her squeal when he suddenly rolled her to her back. "That grin was downright wicked," he murmured in her ear as he placed her thighs over his hips.

She crossed her ankles on his back and nipped at his earlobe, then whispered, "I'll show you downright wicked."

"Please, I'm all yours."

And he was. Thrusting inside her, holding her against him in a way he knew would bring her to a shattering climax. She felt the climb begin, slowly and deliciously, and sunk into it until the pressure grew so intense she screamed when he took her over the edge into release. Even then, she knew just how to lift, to tighten...and take him over the edge with her.

They were both panting, their skin sheened with

sweat when some semblance of normalcy returned to her. "How do you do that?"

She expected a grin and a smart-ass answer, but he was silent, his expression...she wasn't quite sure what that expression was. She'd never seen it before. Well, maybe once. On the dance floor.

"Stay with me, Sunny."

"I wasn't planning on leaving. At least not immediately, anyway."

"I don't mean just for tonight."

Oh. Oh, God! "What— What exactly are you asking me? To...move in or...or something?"

Suddenly she wasn't at all sure she wanted to hear what he was going to say. She was hoping for little steps, a revealing of their true feelings, then a prolonged discussion of what that meant, followed by days, weeks maybe, of talking about the next step. But that wasn't going to happen. It was all going to happen now. And she wasn't ready!

Nick rolled to his side and drew her with him, so her head was pillowed beside his chest. He propped himself on one elbow and gazed into her eyes. "Sunny, I've been thinking about you...about us...a lot this past week or so. I know we said this was only going to be a fling, something for fun, before you went...before you went back home."

There was a bleakness in his eyes when he said that. She reached up and stroked his face. "It was supposed to be just for fun." She ran her thumb over his lips. "So, now what do we do?"

"Just tell me one thing."

"What?"

"Tell me that you'll stay long enough for us to find out what we really want."

"I'm not ready to make promises, Nick," she murmured, hating to cause him any pain, but knowing she had to be completely honest with him.

"But—"

"But we have time before I'm supposed to be anywhere other than right here. Plenty of time to talk about things and make plans and do all that deciding. Just not right now, okay?"

She hated the worry she saw creep into his eyes, but he knew her well enough not to push.

"Okay. But I won't promise that after our dramatic exit back there my family hasn't already booked the church and hired the band."

Her heart raced at the thought. He hadn't told her he loved her, much less proposed marriage, but she couldn't stop the vision anyway. A lovely church wedding with all of Nick's family and friends around her. That her own family didn't enter into her lovely little dream she couldn't face right now. So what if she wanted to dream impossible dreams and allow her heart to fly a bit? Reality would always be there to bring it back. Probably with a painful thud.

All those thoughts flitted away as Nick began the most delectable nibbling along her neck.

"Since we're not going to spend the rest of what is left of tonight talking, I do have several other options I'm willing to discuss."

Sunny squirmed as his hands slid down her back and beneath the covers. "I might be willing to settle on a merger acquisition," she said. The rest was lost on a long moan of delight.

Nick laughed, then disappeared beneath the covers.

Sunny's back arched, and all thoughts of what she'd do with her life beyond the next electrifying hour dissolved.

NICK SHOULD HAVE been disgusted with himself. He walked around the back of his car to open the door for Sunny, hating that he couldn't touch her for those five seconds it took to get out of the car and open her door. Besotted was putting it mildly. And yet, when she smiled at him as she offered him her hand to help her out, he thought besotted was a great state to be in. The whole world should be so lucky to be as besotted as he was.

He'd meant to tell her he loved her last night, had every intention of doing just that when they'd left the festival. But he'd known after asking her to stay with him that she wasn't ready to hear those words. Actually, he was still shocked at how badly he'd wanted to say them. But here it was, the next morning, and he still felt that way.

She stepped to the curb and went to move past him, but he took her into his arms, not caring if Mr. Bertolucci was watching.

She rolled her eyes as he wrapped his arms around her. "Boy, just in case carrying me off last night didn't do the trick, huh?"

He almost told her right then, but he knew she needed him to tease right back, to not pressure her beyond what his family was already doing. Or was going to do. God help them both after his little demonstration last night. Still, he couldn't resist doing a little more than teasing. He bent her back over his knee and kissed her with all the love he felt, then smiled a bit sheepishly as two of the neighboring store owners applauded when he stood Sunny up, albeit a bit wobbly, on her feet. "Show's over, folks," he called, but winked at a blushing Sunny. He straightened the collar of her shirt. "Are you ready?"

She took a deep breath and nodded. "As I'll ever be. There's no banner draped across the restaurant, so that's a good sign, right?"

Nick laughed. She'd handle it okay. Question was, would he? He grasped her hand and held it tight as they walked in the back door.

"I'm just going to run upstairs and change, then I'll meet you in your office, okay?"

He had paperwork to do, invoices to check and an

order to fill out, all before starting the day's work. What he really wanted to do, though, was climb those stairs behind her and crawl into bed with her.

"Sunny? Nicco? Is that you?"

"Should I make a run for it?" Sunny said, laughing.

Mama Bennie's stout figure came into view as she turned the hallway corner. "There you are!"

"Too late now," Nick said out of the side of his mouth to Sunny, just before being engulfed in a big hug.

Sunny's answer, if she'd had one, was muffled against Mama Bennie's ample bosom, as she, too, was engulfed in a big hug.

Bennie eyed them both. "So, do you have any news to share with an old woman who doesn't have too many more years and would like to hold her oldest grandson's babies in her lap before the good Lord calls her home?"

Sunny choked, and Nick groaned. "Bennie, please."

She looked properly affronted. "These days young people don't understand from subtlety. A waste of time in my book, anyhow." She clasped her hands and looked at them expectantly, but there was something else in her dark eyes. Uncertainty?

"Is something else going on?" Nick asked.

Her clasped hands were twisted together. "I was hoping to hear good news, that is all. Before..." She looked over her shoulder, then sighed so heavily her frame appeared suddenly curved, as if carrying an immense burden.

Alarmed, Nick put his arm around her shoulder. Sunny drew closer, as well. "What's wrong?"

She looked over her shoulder once again, then took Sunny's hand and squeezed it. "Your grandmother is here. She wouldn't tell me why she'd come, but she wants to see you. I called Niccolo's place, but you two had already left." She paused, her eyes full of concern. "I made her some tea. She's waiting for you out front."

Nick saw that Sunny was standing still as a stone, her eyes hollow with concern...and fear. Just as quickly she pulled herself together and gave Mama Bennie a reassuring kiss on the cheek. "It's okay. I understand. Please, don't worry." She straightened and looked at Nick. "I guess I'd better go see what she wants."

"Sunny—" He didn't want to let her go. To his surprise, it wasn't for selfish reasons. It frightened him in a way he'd never felt before. What happened in the next couple of minutes could have an impact on his whole life. So it was normal that he'd want to go with her and do whatever he could to make it work to his advantage.

But that wasn't what was keeping his grip on her hand so firm. He wanted to go with her to support her. In whatever happened, whatever the outcome.

He didn't want her to face what was probably going to be a very difficult conversation alone.

"It's probably best I see what she wants. I'll come back to your office as soon as we're done and tell you everything. Okay?"

No, it wasn't okay, he wanted to shout. None of this was. He just found her, just realized he wanted to keep her forever. And now...what? Now it might all be over before it began?

"Trust me, Nick." She looked directly into his eyes.

She was right. The whole reason she'd come into his life in the first place was so she could decide for herself what she wanted. If he didn't trust her to choose on her own, then he was no better than her family, making important decisions for her.

But it didn't make it any easier to let go of her hand. "If you need me, or want me for any reason, you know where I'll be." *Pacing my office like a caged animal, waiting to hear what my fate will be.*

She kissed him, right there in front of Bennie and everything. "Thank you, Nick. For understanding me better than anyone ever has."

He swallowed hard, then watched her walk away from him.

Mama Bennie grabbed his hand and squeezed it. "She'll do the right thing, our Sunny. She's a strong one."

Knowing his doubts showed on his face, Nick said softly, "I hope so, Mama. I hope so."

13

SPYING HER GRANDMOTHER sitting stiffly at one of the small tables near the door, Sunny paused, taken aback.

She looked...frail. A trait Sunny could never remember associating with Frances Chandler. Although her posture was as erect as ever, there was an air of defeat about her elegantly attired frame.

Anxiety filled Sunny, and she hurried across the room. "Grandmother?"

It only took one look into Frances's pale blue eyes to confirm her fears. Something was wrong. Terribly wrong.

"Please sit down, Susan. There is something I must discuss with you."

Sunny's throat tightened as she sat across from her. "What's wrong?"

"It's Edwin. He's had...a setback."

"Is he okay?" Sunny's voice trembled. She restrained her impulse to take her grandmother's hand or in some way give her comfort. And get comfort in return. Instead, knowing her grandmother would strongly disapprove of any public display, Sunny folded her hands in her lap.

"He's home now."

Sunny released a silent sigh of relief. She was upset that she hadn't been contacted sooner. He'd obviously spent time in the hospital. There was no use in belaboring the point. Frances may be hiding it well, but Sunny saw the toll this turn of events had taken on her.

Sunny's hands coiled into tight fists from the tension of holding back. She was suddenly struck by how profoundly she'd changed these past few weeks. Being around the D'Angelo family had given her the freedom to openly express her needs and desires. It had already become second nature to her to touch, to reach out, to comfort. To expect it in return.

Sitting here with her grandmother, she realized she couldn't go back to her old way of being. She couldn't go back to doing what was expected of her at the expense of her own needs. And those of the people she loved. The very idea made her stomach hurt.

And yet, wasn't that what she was already doing?

Well, no more. Very deliberately she reached over and covered her grandmother's hand with her own, giving it a gentle squeeze. Frances stiffened, and her eyes widened in disapproval, but Sunny noted with a warm surge of satisfaction that she didn't remove her hand.

"What's happened?" Sunny asked. "How long was his stay in the hospital?" *Was it my fault?*

Frances pursed her lips, and Sunny's heart dipped when her grandmother removed her hand to take a slow sip of her tea. It was a polite pause designed to allow Sunny to gain control over her emotions, to behave appropriately. To do the right thing.

Sunny had never felt so wrong in her life. She didn't want to sit there and quietly inquire as to the state of her grandfather's health. She wanted to race out the door, Frances in tow, grab the first taxi and rush to his side.

But despite Sunny's vow to change things, there were some things that would never be changed. "Please," Sunny said, trying to keep the resignation from her tone, "just tell me what happened."

Frances carefully set her teacup on its saucer before answering. "His cardiologist is afraid he has been placing too much strain on his heart these past several months. This merger has been complicated and he's been spending an inordinate amount of time on it."

Sunny couldn't stop guilt from flooding through her. Even she wasn't that strong. Her grandfather had wanted her there to help with this merger, and she'd gone off on her own instead.

"But he's so strong," she murmured. Her eyes watered as she looked into the steady gaze of her grandmother. "Will he fully recover?"

"With bed rest and diet, he should make a full re-
covery." She seemed to sit a bit straighter, her composure seemingly bolstered in direct opposition to
Sunny losing hers. "It's time for you to come home,
Susan. You must take your rightful place as Edwin's
heir. There is still much that has to be done, and Edwin will not rest if someone other than a Chandler is
at the helm."

Sunny felt overwhelmed by feelings of obligation...and entrapment. Certainly she must return
home. She'd known this moment was coming all
along, albeit not for this reason. But she wasn't ready.
She simply wasn't ready.

And yet, what choice did she have?

"I have a car waiting outside. If you could just
gather your things, we'll be on our way."

Sunny's eyes widened. "I can't simply walk away.
I have responsibilities here."

Her grandmother eyed her. "Having responsibilities didn't seem to be a concern one month ago."

Sunny reminded herself that she was a grown
woman with her own mind and that it was her choice
what she would or wouldn't do. But Frances knew
precisely what button to push. Sunny's guilt button
was glowing a bright neon red at the moment. And
knowing she was being manipulated didn't lessen
the feeling.

"I need to go and explain what has happened."
When her grandmother didn't so much as blink,

Sunny's resolve began to return. Frances *had* raised her, and Sunny had learned a thing or two from her despite herself. "I have several other things to take care of, as well. Then I'd like to go see Grandfather. Afterward I'll need to come back here and pack up. I'll return to Haddon Hall as quickly as I can after that." If her grandmother noticed she hadn't referred to Haddon Hall as home, she didn't let it show. Sunny wondered what she would say if she told Frances D'Angelos had come to be more of a home to her in one month than the place she'd spent almost her entire life.

Her grandmother's expression remained impassive, but Sunny felt the displeasure emanating from her nonetheless.

"I'm afraid we'll need you at Chandler Enterprises immediately. Edwin is resting. You can visit him later when he is up to it." She paused, then said, "I will arrange to send someone for your things." She glanced around, and had she allowed such things, Sunny was certain she would have given a visible shudder. As it was, there was no question Frances disapproved of her even being here, much less working and living here.

Angry at her grandmother's dismissive attitude toward Sunny's responsibilities to the D'Angelos, she refused to give in to her wishes and shelve her own— yet again. She stood. "Thank you for your kind offer. However, I will come back and take care of things here myself." She lifted a hand when Frances started to rebut her decision.

"I won't shirk my responsibility to Chandler Enterprises." If she didn't stand her ground now, then this past month would have been for nothing. It wasn't how she planned on returning, but she'd be damned if she'd go back to being the obedient little Susan they expected her to be. "However, I made it clear to Grandfather when I left that I needed this time for myself. I owe you and Grandfather a debt I cannot possibly repay, but despite what has happened, I do not think asking for some time before dedicating the remainder of my life to the company was asking too much. I made the decision to come here, and I have not regretted one minute of the time I've spent. Like it or not, there are other people who count on me now, as well."

After collecting her purse, Frances rose. "Your grandfather is expecting your appearance at Chandler Enterprises shortly. From his sick bed, he has arranged for a board meeting and extensive briefing to take place within the hour. Arrive promptly."

Sunny said nothing. With a hollow pit in her stomach, she watched her grandmother depart. Carl leapt to attention and helped Frances into the back seat of the company limo.

Frances might be shaken up by Edwin's sudden health problems—although no one but Sunny would have been able to tell—but she was not going to step back and allow Sunny to call the shots. Edwin might be the power at Chandler Enterprises, but Frances was the ruler of the personal Chandler empire. Her will would not be easily deterred.

Sunny was trembling as she watched the limo drive away from the curb. She turned to look around the restaurant. So, she was going home. Why did it feel like she was about to leave it, instead?

With a heart heavier than she could ever remember, she headed to the office, to Nick and Mama Bennie.

She knocked lightly on the door, and it swung open before she could reach for the knob. Nick immediately took her into his arms and kissed her. She should push away. It wasn't fair to either of them to carry on with this. But she couldn't. She wanted to be held by him, kissed senseless by him, at least this one last time. Surely it wasn't wrong to allow herself a goodbye kiss?

Nick was the one to break it off, and even before she glanced at his face, she could feel by the tightening of his body that he knew what she was going to say. What she had no choice but to say.

"I'm so sorry, Nick," she whispered. She raised her teary eyes to his, dark and intense as ever.

"You don't have to go, Sunny."

"Nick—" She paused, took a deep, calming breath, then let it out slowly. She had to get through this without falling apart. Things were about to get a whole lot harder for her, and she'd have to find a way to handle them. "My grandfather is very ill."

The fingers that had been holding her shoulders immediately relaxed into a massaging motion. "Oh, Sunny. I'm so sorry."

Strangely, it was his instant understanding that almost destroyed what little control she had left. He would understand this more than anyone. It was family, and when family needed you, you went. "It's not when or how I'd have chosen to do this." He was looking at her with so damn much compassion and affection and— "Maybe it's for the best."

He frowned, and she saw the heat behind the compassion. "There is nothing remotely best about you leaving."

Her mouth dropped open as he tugged her close. But no words came out. This was not what she'd expected.

"Sunny, what we have together is no fling."

She looked away, unable to face the pain she saw creeping into his eyes.

He gently tipped her chin up. "Just because you're going back to help out while your grandfather is getting better...does that mean we have to end this? End us?"

My God. He wasn't going to let her go. Suddenly, despite all the tumultuous feelings rocketing through her...she found herself smiling. "Boy, Frances isn't going to approve of this at all."

"That's a yes?"

"That's a yes."

Nick yanked her against him, his kiss more demanding and honest than any they'd shared before. And when she opened her eyes and the room stopped spinning, Nick was still there, standing before her. Steady as always, there for her to lean on, to take strength from.

Doubt suddenly rushed in. Was she merely substituting the crutch of her family's demands for the crutch of Nick's strength?

"Don't," he warned.

She blinked. "Don't what?"

"Don't start second-guessing."

"I'm not."

"Yes, you are. I know you, Sunny."

It was another moment of revelation for her. He did know her. The real her. And he wanted the real her, faults and all.

"I want to make sure I am standing on my own two feet," she said. "I need to know I'm able to do this on my own."

"Okay. If I walked away right now, told you I never wanted to see you again, would you still be able to go back to Chandler Enterprises and do what you have to do?"

Just hearing him say he never wanted to see her again made her heart throb with hurt. "Yes," she said softly. "But I—"

"And when you said you wanted to keep seeing me, was it because you thought that was what *I* wanted?"

"No. I mean, I do think you want me to keep seeing you, but I said yes because it was what I wanted, too."

"Then what's the problem?"

She blew out a long sigh.

"You don't have to deal with this entirely on your own, you know."

"Yes, I do. I have to. There is no one else to do it."

"There might not be someone else to go into that boardroom for you, but there is someone who wants to hear all about it afterward."

"Nick, that's—" She hesitated as his words sunk in. "Wait a minute. How do you know about the board meeting?"

His smile was charmingly sheepish. "Well, I might be strong enough to stay back here while you fight your own dragons—and let me tell you, your grandmother throws quite a mean flame—but that didn't mean I wasn't prepared to let you get toasted without even trying to save you. If you needed me to, that is."

She should be mad at him, but she wasn't. There was something quite wonderful about knowing someone cared about her that much.

"If it makes you feel any better, I tried to stay in my office."

"Lasted five minutes, did you?"

He grinned. "At the most." Then he grew more serious. "I am sorry to hear about your grandfather. I missed that part. I know all about obligations, but I want you to remember something, Sunny. No matter what they've done for you, given to you, that still does not give them the right to tell you what you will do with the rest of your life."

"I know that, Nick. Being here, with you and your family, has shown me that there is more to life than I ever knew. But being around your family has also shown me how important family is. I know it seems like they don't deserve my dedication, but maybe it's because I've never let them know what I really want from them, what I need. I plan to change that, to not do things I'm uncomfortable with because it makes them comfortable or because it's expected of me. I don't know what I can change, or even if I can change them at all. But I can change me, and I have. Whatever else I've learned, I do know I can't turn my back on the only family I have. Not now."

Nick didn't say anything for a long moment, then he brushed his fingers over her lips and very softly said, "You have family here now, too. Don't turn your back on us, either."

"I don't want to, Nick." She framed his face with her hands and kissed him, pouring everything she felt into it, her fears, her confusion...her hopes.

They were speechless when the kiss ended. Sunny rested her head on his shoulder. "You know," she said at length, "if anything, I'm being selfish, not ending this right now."

He nuzzled her neck. "I already told you I think you need to be more selfish."

"You have no idea what you're getting into, with my family, I mean. My grandfather's ideas about how the world runs are pretty definite. And my grandmother...well, I'll warn you now, she won't like the idea of you and me together."

Nick leaned back so he could look directly into her eyes. "*Mi cara mia*, if you can survive my family, I think it's only fair I be expected to survive yours."

Sunny didn't know whether to laugh or cry. She still had reservations about not ending this right now. She was only doing this to please herself. But maybe, considering what she faced, she damn well deserved at least that.

14

SHE WAS GONE. Nick stared blindly at the columns of numbers on the spreadsheet in front of him. He knew she was only a phone call away, less than a twenty-minute drive. It didn't help. She wasn't here. She wasn't upstairs playing with one of his nieces, or in the kitchen swearing under her breath in perfect Italian. She wasn't in his arms, in his bed, within his reach.

And there wasn't a damn thing he could do about it.

He knew he should be thanking his lucky stars she hadn't chosen to end their relationship completely, but he was having a hard time feeling generous at the moment. He wanted—

What did he want?

B.J. barged into his office.

"Don't you ever knock?"

"Not since you walked in on me in the bathroom the day I was trying on my first bra, nope."

"Boy, talk about holding a grudge."

"Well, if you hadn't gone and explained, in excruciating detail, just what it looked like to Bobby Tannenhall, I would have forgiven you sooner."

Nick's mood was improving. "Imagine if he could see you now," he said, motioning to her bustline, which had expanded exponentially with her growing belly.

"Ha, ha. Very funny."

A distraction was what he needed. And that was the one thing his sisters could usually be guaranteed to provide. "So, what's up?"

She carefully sat across from him, her expression turning serious. "I wanted to talk to you about Sunny."

He groaned silently. Not the distraction he was hoping for. "What about her?" He knew that with B.J. there would be no use trying to evade the topic. It was best to get it over with.

"We miss her."

Like I don't? he wanted to shout. His head started to pound.

"All of us, Nick. The kids, everyone. She's like a part of the family now."

"She has her own family, Beej. Her grandfather is sick, and she had to go back to help her grandmother."

"Then she'll come back, right?"

Nick refrained from swearing, barely. "I don't know. I know her family wants her to work for the company." Hell, they wanted her to run the damn company. He looked right at B.J. and gave voice to his greatest fear. "She might not come back. Ever."

"Well, that's unacceptable. You have to do something."

He laughed, but there was no humor in it. "B.J., she's a grown woman. An adult with obligations to other people besides us. Even if there was something I could do, I wouldn't. It wouldn't be fair to her."

His baby sister was quiet for a moment. "But what if she really wanted you to?"

Nick sat back in his chair. "I'm not sure what you're getting at here. Sunny has to make her own choices. She doesn't want me or anyone else making them for her."

B.J. stood and leaned her formidable bulk across his desk. "She's letting her family make her choices for her and she's miserable with them. She's happier here. So, as long as she's going to please other people, why not please you. And us. In the end, it will please her, too."

"It scares me when your logic begins to make sense." He stood up. He needed to get out of here, clear his head before he started believing his sister might have a good point.

She put her hand on his arm. "Think about it, Nick. She's unhappy."

"Would you have liked it if we interfered when you decided to marry John?"

She didn't look at all abashed. In fact, she smacked

him and laughed. "What do you mean? You did try to stop me! And you love John, so that won't fly."

"Well, it was for your own good. You were too young."

"What do you know about how I felt?"

"Exactly." He smiled when he saw understanding dawn on her face. "How do you know what Sunny really feels? She loves her family, too. She's in a very difficult spot, and I refuse to add more pressure." He kissed his sister's cheek.

"What was that for?"

"For caring. About Sunny. And about me." He squeezed her shoulders. "As hard as it is, we have to let her make her own choices."

B.J. frowned even as she nodded in agreement. Then she looked at him, more serious than he ever recalled her looking, and said, "But you can't just step back and let her family overwhelm her. If she's going to make a choice, she has to have one to make. At least let her know how you feel, Nick. Let her know what she's choosing between." She lifted a hand when he tried to speak. "I'm not saying pressure her to pick you. I'm just saying, don't let her go without a fight. Maybe she needs to know that. That she's important enough to fight for."

Joey chose that moment to barge in. "Hey, Nicco! And the baby-making machine. What's up?" He slapped Nick on the shoulder and laid a wet, smacking kiss on his slightly older sister's cheek. "Why does everyone look so depressed? Something happen?"

"Sunny's gone," B.J. said flatly. "I'm just making sure this big lug here realizes what he's letting slip away."

"I know she's gone from here," Joey said. "That's why I'm back. I need to sublet my apartment again. And thanks, everyone, for asking about me and telling me how missed I was, by the way."

Nick and B.J. rolled their eyes.

"I don't see the problem," Joey insisted. "She's still in Chicago, right? Can't she work at Chandler's and still hang out with us?"

"That's the plan," Nick said.

Joey shrugged. "Then go with the flow, my man."

"So says the sage twenty-one-year-old." B.J. laughed dryly. "Oh, to be so young and naive again."

Joey rolled his eyes. "I get no respect." He kissed his sister again and punched Nick in the chest, then said, "I'm off to see Mama Bennie. She'll be happy to see me."

Nick rubbed his chest as Joey banged out the door. "What if he's right?"

"Oh, please. Joey's idea of romancing a woman is to spring for two hot dogs from Pete down on Second."

"I'm serious. Maybe it will work."

"She's been gone six days."

"Seven."

"Okay, seven. You want to give me the hours and minutes, too?"

Nick grinned despite himself. "Don't be a smart-ass." But he could have told her to the second, and they both knew it.

"So, she's been gone seven days, and exactly how many times have you seen her?"

"None. But that's not her fault," he added quickly. "She's had to take on an enormous responsibility right away with the merger, and there's no spare time right now. But that will change."

"Will it?"

Nick opened his mouth, then shut it again. Finally, he said, "I hope so, Beej. I hope so."

It was his sister's turn to stand on her toes and strain past her belly to kiss her brother's cheek. "Make sure of it, okay? Like I said, don't just let her disappear. You deserve her, Niccolo. And more important, she deserves you. Don't forget that. She's the one. You know it, we all know it. If you don't at least try, you'll never forgive yourself."

Nick watched his sister walk out of his office, but he didn't move for several long moments.

You'll never forgive yourself.

"Yeah," he said softly, "but what if I try, and fail. I'm not sure I'll forgive myself for that, either."

SUNNY MADE SURE the door was locked before she kicked her heels halfway across the ocean of blue Aubusson that carpeted her office floor. If she thought it wouldn't bring all three of her secretaries and her personal executive assistant running, she'd have given a good long primal scream, as well.

"Torture," she muttered. "Pure torture." She wondered what the executive heads of Chandler's sundry branches would think if she decided to wear her comfortable black kitchen shoes from D'Angelos. Even picturing the polite distaste on their pinched faces did little to improve her mood. "Stubborn sons of—" She bit off the last part, a groan of relief slipping out as she rubbed her feet.

Even as she worked the kinks out of her toes, her mind was buzzing with possible solutions to the latest round of problems with the merger. She needed to get that report from Roger and then have a talk with Estelle and Paul before the meeting this afternoon. She glanced at the clock and realized lunch had come and gone again, and made another mental note to start penciling in working lunches. She spent a second fantasizing about Carlo's fettucine, then a solution to the human resource department problem popped into her mind and she shuttled to her desk and started making notes.

Thirty minutes and six phone calls later she came up for air again. She had two hours before the meeting with the corporate heads and her grandfather had requested a phone conference to discuss strategy beforehand. She glanced at her calendar and picked up the phone to call Nick, then realized he would be in the middle of his weekly staff meeting and put the phone down.

She massaged her temples, letting her mind stray to dangerous territory. Nick. She missed him terribly. As she did the rest of the D'Angelo family. Haddon Hall had never felt colder. Which was why she put in sixteen-hour days at Chandler's. It wasn't family here, unless you called minnows and sharks a family, but here she could stay busy enough to not have to think about Nick. And the choices she had to make.

She missed him. She wanted him as much if not more than she had the day she left D'Angelos. She had known time off would be a rare commodity, and they'd discussed that. Nick had been more understanding than she might have been if their situations were reversed, and yet he'd given every indication that he was still interested in pursuing their relationship. He didn't pressure her...and maybe a part of her wished he would. But there was another part of her that was relieved. And that was precisely what she'd been trying to ignore.

She'd expected the immense workload, the loneliness. What she hadn't counted on was that, except for that last part...she liked it. No. She had to be honest. She loved it. Thrived on it. As much as it pained her to admit it—to herself and to her grandparents— they'd been right. She was cut out for this.

But how could she tell Nick?

This wasn't going to be a short-term thing where her work schedule would let up after the merger. If anything, it would get busier. The challenge energized her like nothing in her life ever had. Except perhaps her feelings for Nick.

So, what was she going to do? She couldn't expect Nick to wait around for the crumbs of time she could give him, nor would she want him to. But she didn't want him to leave, either. The very idea of never seeing him again was too painful to imagine. She wanted—

What did she want?

She knew what she wanted. She wanted it all. And, as of right now, she had not one clue how she could make that happen. Which was why she'd focused on work instead.

Her intercom buzzed, startling her out of her troubled thoughts. She pressed the button. "Yes, Peggy?"

"Mrs. Chandler here to see you, ma'am."

Grandmother? Sunny hadn't worked here long, but she had lived at Haddon Hall almost her entire life, and as far as she knew, Frances ruled the roost there and let Edwin rule his empire here. The twain rarely met.

"Send her in."

She automatically smoothed her hair and winced as she shoved her toes into her shoes. She was halfway to the door when Frances entered. Sunny faltered before continuing.

"Grandmother, what a nice surprise." Sunny didn't have to look very hard to see the lines of fatigue and worry in her grandmother's normally calm and collected expression.

"Can I get you some tea?"

"No, thank you, Susan. I need to discuss something with you."

Sunny gave her grandmother a peck on the cheek and a light hug, something she'd been making Frances endure ever since her return from D'Angelos, but the older woman smoothly bypassed Sunny and crossed to the small grouping of stuffed leather chairs that fronted a monstrosity of a fireplace opposite her desk.

Frances sat, her bearing as regal as a queen's, awaiting Sunny's compliance with her forthcoming decree.

Suppressing a sigh of disappointment, Sunny crossed the room and sat in the chair opposite her grandmother. "What do you need to discuss with me?" she inquired politely. She was too tired to press her own agenda. She'd play Frances's way this time around.

"The gala we're having with the Madison people."

Sunny nodded, though she was baffled why Frances was mentioning this, much less making the trip to do it in person. Chandler was hosting the function so that the corporate heads of both merging companies could meet on a social level. The hope, of course, was that some of the more delicate kinks in the business deal could be worked out over hors d'oeuvres and champagne.

"I'm not sure what it is I can do to help. Is it the guest list?"

"Heavens, no. That was taken care of months ago."

Sunny waited, but Frances was silent. Sunny had no idea what she was expected to say. "Are you certain I can't get you some tea?" Rule number one in polite society—when in doubt, serve something.

"Perhaps I will. Thank you."

Sunny went to her desk, her mind rifling through all the possible reasons for her grandmother being here. She discreetly buzzed for Peggy to bring them tea. As soon as she sat down again, the answer hit her like a ton of bricks.

"Grandfather. Has something happened?"

For the first time in possibly Frances's entire life, certainly for as long as Sunny had been alive, Frances's expression crumpled. Sunny was out of her seat in a shot, kneeling in front of her grandmother, taking her hands. They were icy and tight with tension.

"What's happened?" She rubbed her grandmother's hands, hoping to give her some warmth and comfort. "Is he all right?"

Frances struggled to compose herself, but even though she regained control of her facial expression, her eyes mirrored abject fear. "He's had...another setback." Her voice was shaky, and Sunny was afraid she was going to cry.

She'd never understood just how much she relied on her grandmother to be an anchor, perpetually composed in the face of every obstacle. In that moment, she felt petty and horribly selfish for wanting Frances to be all that and warm and loving, too. She'd never realized how much of her strength and balance she'd gotten from the woman whose hands she was clinging to.

"He's back in the hospital. They say he'll be fine, but—" Her voice caught, and Sunny watched her fierce struggle for control. She could only guess at how mortifying this was for Frances, and immediately did what she could to preserve what was left of her grandmother's dignity.

Sunny stood and returned to her desk, punching the button for Peggy. "Have them bring Mrs. Chandler's car around to the private entrance, please. Thank you, Peggy."

She turned to her grandmother, who was standing, but looking a bit lost. "Susan—"

"I want you to go be with Grandfather. Just tell me who I need to talk to about the gala and I'll make certain all the details are taken care of."

Her grandmother nodded, then her shoulders straightened and she crossed to the door, gloves and purse in hand. She turned. "I'll leave the list with your secretary."

"Good."

Frances started to open the door, then stopped and looked at Sunny. There was a fine tremor in her voice when she spoke. "Thank you, Susan. We're very proud of you, Edwin and I. You've grown into such a fine, accomplished woman. We always knew we could count on you to do the right thing. And you've done it very well."

On a whisper of silk, she was gone.

Stunned, Sunny sat on her desk and burst into tears.

15

SUNNY PACED the Haddon Hall ballroom, the click of her heels echoing on the inlaid wood floor. She tried to focus on the upcoming gala event and the myriad details she was responsible for. However, the solution to her biggest problem was due to arrive any minute, and that was all she could think about.

Nick.

She hadn't seen him in two weeks. Had barely talked to him in the past five days. The deeper she sank into the chaotic, exciting affairs of Chandler Enterprises, the more she worried that her relationship with Nick was over.

Until she was given what she hoped was a reprieve. Now came the hard part. She had to find out if he still wanted to make it work as badly as she did. She no longer had any idea. She thought back to their last night together. The festival seemed so long ago...and just like yesterday, all at the same time. She remembered that look in his eyes, both on the dance floor and after they'd made love. She'd tortured herself with it many times. Had he intended to tell her he loved her? Had her insecurities kept him from saying it? And now...despite telling her he didn't want to end it, was he glad he'd never said those words?

Vincent, the Chandlers' houseman, stepped quietly into the room. "Your guest has arrived, miss."

"Show him in, Vincent."

"It's a her, miss. Madame D'Angelo."

Sunny's heart sank. She missed Nick's sisters terribly, but she thought they'd understand just how disappointed she was at that moment. But it was Mama Bennie who stepped into the ballroom. She was using her cane, and made her way slowly into the room.

"Mama Bennie, what a nice surprise."

"I know you were expecting Niccolo, but there was a problem with Carlo that he had to see to personally, so I decided to come for him." She looked around. "Quite the dance hall you have here."

Sunny grinned. "We're party animals, us Chandlers." She was terribly disappointed that Nick wasn't coming, but when Mama Bennie folded her into her arms for a warm hug and kiss, Sunny felt tears spring to her eyes. "I've missed you," she said emotionally.

"We all miss you, too, Sunny. When are you coming home?"

Well, nothing like getting to the heart of the matter. Sunny took a breath and gestured toward the arrangement of chairs in the corner near the French doors. "Why don't we have a seat."

"I understand you need some help."

Sunny settled into her chair, knowing Bennie hadn't forgotten her last question, but grateful she was going to be given a reprieve. For the moment anyway. "My grandfather has taken a turn for the worse. He'll be fine, but he's back in the hospital. Frances is being pulled in too many directions and so I agreed to take on helping with the big gala she is organizing to celebrate the merger going through."

"I'm sorry to hear about Edwin, dear," Bennie said, reaching over to pat her hand.

Sunny must be more stressed than she'd thought. All Bennie had to do was touch her and the waterworks threatened. It was all she could do not to fling herself at Bennie and sob about how badly she'd missed them all and beg her to help her find a solution to all her problems with her relationship with Nick.

Calling on all of Frances's formidable training, she managed to smile calmly instead. "Thank you."

"What do you need us for?"

Everything. She almost said it out loud. How had she survived without their loving warmth these past two weeks? The answer was—barely.

"We've used the same caterer for years and had retained them for this function, as well," Sunny said, "but I found out this morning that the head chef has quit and run off with the owner's wife."

Bennie's eyes twinkled. "Interesting turn of events."

Sunny felt a little stress leave her. "Yes. And as much as I hate to impose on you, I need some help."

For the first time since coming in the room, Bennie frowned. "You're like family to us, Sunny. We'd be hurt if you went elsewhere. I take it you need someone to cater this little event of yours."

"It's a gala. Two hundred people. In two weeks." She winced, waiting.

Bennie simply smiled. "We've handled worse." She shifted in her seat. "Have you told your grandmother?"

Sunny didn't have to ask what she meant. D'Angelos might have been the number-one choice to cater weddings, communions, wakes and the like in their own neighborhood, but it was quite a different matter here. She held Bennie's gaze and said, "Frances left me in charge of this shindig. I'll handle things as I see fit, and she'll just have to deal with it. If she doesn't like how I've taken care of things, then she'll find someone else next time."

Bennie tapped her cane on the floor and smiled. "That's our Sunny." She reached over and patted Sunny's knee. "We'll take care of it."

She blew out a sigh of relief. "Thank you, Mama Bennie. You don't know what this means to me."

"It means you know who to ask when you need help. Now, why don't you ask me about Niccolo."

Sunny sputtered for a moment, caught off guard.

The twinkle in Bennie's eyes told her that was exactly what she'd meant to do.

"The boy mopes and pouts and is horribly short-tempered with the kitchen help."

Sunny laughed even as her heart skipped a beat or two. "He's not. He's the most patient man I know."

Bennie's gaze steadied on hers. "He won't wait forever, Sunny."

Sunny's heart tightened inside her chest. "I'm not asking him to."

"Well, what are you asking him to do, then?"

She honestly didn't know what to say.

Bennie shifted forward in her seat and took Sunny's hand. "I might be an old woman, Sunny, but I know true love when I see it. Don't let him get away from you. You're the best thing that's ever happened to him." She squeezed her hand. "And we're the best thing that's ever happened to you." She released Sunny's hand and stood with surprising ease. "Don't you forget that. Now, who do I talk to in this museum about the guest lists and all that?"

Sunny managed to get to her feet and press the button to page Vincent, but he was ever so efficiently there before she could say anything.

"Yes, miss?"

"Could you show Mrs. D'Angelo to Mary Anne's office?" She turned to Bennie and impulsively threw her arms around her and hugged her. "You are the best thing, Mama Bennie," she whispered in her ear.

"You all are. And I won't ever forget all that you've done for me. All that you've been for me."

Sunny ignored Vincent's disapproving expression as he crossed the room to escort Bennie to Frances's assistant's office. "If there are any questions, please just call me."

But Bennie was already talking to Vincent, asking about his family and where he was from. Sunny sat in her chair. Once again a family matriarch had left her reeling.

TWO WEEKS. Nick paced the serving hall. It had been two weeks since Sunny had contracted D'Angelos to cater their gala. Two weeks of rushed phone calls and increasing frustration at the direction their relationship was taking. Most of the details for the event had been handled by Frances's personal assistant, so even that hadn't brought them closer together. Mama Bennie had had nothing but glowing things to say about Sunny and how she'd come to family when she needed them.

Nick wished like hell she'd come to him. He sure as hell needed her. She might as well be on another continent. He knew she was swamped, knew just how overwhelmed she was. And if she'd sounded excited and energized by the whole ordeal...well, Nick was trying not to think about that part too hard. The fact was, he'd been busier than normal, too. Carlo had told him he was going to retire at the end of the summer, and Nick had no idea how he was going to replace him. B.J. was having some complications with the impending birth of her twins and was at the doctor every other day, it seemed. He felt like he was being yanked in ten different directions.

He should have been glad that Sunny was so busy, taking the pressure off him having to work hard at maintaining a relationship with her, as well. The truth was, it was the exact opposite. He'd needed her. More than ever. The more stress he found himself under, the more he needed to talk things over with her, lean on her a little, draw comfort from her. It should have shocked him more, this neediness. Instead it frustrated him. Frustrated him because he didn't know how to fulfill it.

He hadn't told Sunny about what was going on with Carlo or B.J. She had enough on her plate. And he assumed, knowing her like he did, that she was doing the same with him, not telling him all.

God, he hoped so. Because he'd come to a decision.

After the gala tonight, he was going to find her, and he wasn't about to accept no for an answer. They were going to spend the rest of this night together. He was going to tell her he loved her. And, if he had his way, he was going to find some way to spend the rest of their lives together, too.

There had to be a solution. Living like this, without her, was just not working.

"Please God," he prayed beneath his breath as he

watched the guests begin to file into the ballroom.
"Let her feel the same way."

FOUR HOURS LATER, Nick was ready to admit defeat.
He hadn't had a chance to talk to Sunny, but he'd certainly had plenty of chances to see her. She looked
stunning. Her hair was swept back and up, showing
off the elegant line of her neck and jaw. Her dress was
a strapless number, ice blue, and it fitted her like it
had been made just for her. Which, probably, it had.
She'd smiled, danced and charmed everyone in the
room. The men all wanted to talk to her, the women
wanted to be her. She was in her element.

He'd tried to tell himself that she was merely doing
her familial duty until he'd overheard her talking
shop in the midst of a clutch of penguin-suited gen-
tlemen. Her eyes sparkled. Her voice was passionate.
Her every breath made it clear that she was completely engaged by what she was doing, by her commitment to Chandler Enterprises. She loved it,
thrived on it, if seeing was believing. She'd finally
found her passion.

And even though his heart was taking a bit of a
beating as he watched her, there was no doubting the
other emotion swamping him. Pride. Fierce pride.
That was his Sunny conquering this roomful of
stuffed shirts, his Sunny who had them eating out of
the palm of her manicured and expensively lotioned
hands. His Sunny.

Their Sunny.

Chandler Enterprises had just lucked into its greatest fortune ever. She belonged right here, in this room, with these people, doing what she was born to do. Not because she was supposed to do it, but because she loved it.

He'd already known it. Had heard it in her voice, but didn't want to believe it. He wondered if she knew it, if she'd admitted to herself that this was where she belonged. Not in some sweaty kitchen swearing in cultured Italian, or tucked away in a small apartment in the city with a restaurant owner. No. She belonged right here.

He, on the other hand, did not.

Nick made certain the cleanup crew had arrived and been briefed, made last-minute checks on the wine and champagne count, then went out the service entry of Haddon Hall. He wouldn't be back.

SUNNY finally maneuvered her way from the ballroom on the pretense of checking some problem or other, then ducked into the service entrance to the kitchen. She'd only glimpsed Nick tonight. She'd hoped to have at least a few words with him. Tonight had gone far better than she expected. She'd managed to finagle some last-minute concessions from the Madison CEO, and she'd made damn sure he agreed to a Saturday morning meeting so she could get it in writing. She hurried down the hall into the kitchen, a wide grin she'd been keeping to herself finally plastering itself all over her face. She'd done it!

Edwin would be so proud. Her smile twisted. Okay, so he'd at least be relieved she hadn't screwed things up. She was eager to share her first major corporate victory with the person who mattered most to her.

The swinging door swished shut behind her. "Can you tell me where Nick D'Angelo is, please?" she asked the first person she saw. It must have been a new hire for the night, because she didn't recognize him.

"I'm sorry miss, but he's left for the night. Let me get Louis for you."

She froze, her smile gone in a flash.

"Miss?"

She snapped out of her momentary shock and looked at the waiter. "No, it's not important."

She turned and went out the door. Not important? Like hell it wasn't.

She walked slowly toward the ballroom. The evening was winding down, and she needed to get in there to say good-night to her guests as they departed. Frances was there, but Sunny's absence would be noticed, and she couldn't afford to do anything to jeopardize the victories she'd secured tonight. She'd only wanted to see if Nick would meet her later.

Why had he left without even trying to see her?

Had something come up at the restaurant? This late at night, she doubted it. Maybe he'd thought her too busy to see him. There was a twinge of guilt there. She'd had hardly any time these past weeks, but with the merger now nearly complete, that was all about to change.

She'd made several major decisions of her own.

She entered the ballroom, terrified that she'd let her relationship with Nick slip through her hands when she'd been up to her ears in work.

And yet, three days and three times as many unreturned phone calls later, she was very much afraid that she had.

16

NICK FOLLOWED Vincent into the sitting room at Haddon Hall. Quite a different path than the one he'd exited three days ago. Looking at the antiques and works of art placed just so along the main hallway, he thought his nieces and nephews could cost the Chandlers a fortune in just one visit. Not that this would ever come to pass.

He hadn't intended on coming here again. He was only here because Bennie had left an urgent message saying Frances Chandler or her assistant—he hadn't been completely clear on which—had wanted to see him about some other catering arrangements for some of their gala guests. Nick couldn't believe that Sunny's crowd had suddenly flipped for Italian cuisine, but stranger things had happened. And even if he and Sunny hadn't been able to make a go of it, he was enough of a businessman not to walk away from the possibility of obtaining some new clients.

He only hoped Frances didn't bring up Sunny during their meeting. Nick was well aware Sunny had called a number of times, but he still hadn't figured out what to say to her. Certainly she'd recognized by now that their lives wouldn't mesh. Still, Nick needed to see her and talk to her about...everything. And he would.

Just as soon as he could do it without crawling to her on his hands and knees and begging her to come back to him.

At least she'd be at work at this hour, so he wouldn't end up running into her.

Vincent showed him into a room that was grand even by presidential standards. Hell, royal standards. He declined the seat he was offered.

"Can I get you a drink, sir?"

"No, thanks."

"Ms. Chandler won't be long."

Nick nodded, then scanned the room after Vincent departed. He'd hardly had time to give more than a cursory glance at the furnishings when the door opened again.

"Grandmother, I don't see why we couldn't have— Oh. It's you."

Nick's heart shot into a triple-time beat, and he spun around. His ears hadn't played a trick on him. "Sunny."

She had paused inside the doorway. Wearing a deep blue business suit and with her hair elegantly swept up, she appeared the consummate young professional, cool and entirely capable of handling a boardroom full of stuffed suits twice her age. She looked like Edwin Chandler's granddaughter.

Not Nick D'Angelo's lover. Much less his wife.

He rubbed his damp fingers against his trousers. "I didn't expect to see you here."

She looked just as shell-shocked as he felt. "My grandmother called and asked for a meeting. She said it was urgent."

"I was told that she wanted to see me about something to do with the gala last week."

They both fell silent. Nick mentally cursed the awkwardness that sprang up between them. "Sunny—"

"Nick—"

Nick continued when she didn't. "I need to apologize to you."

She lifted her eyebrow, and he didn't know whether to smile or cry. Damn, but he missed her.

"For?"

"Not returning your calls." He couldn't remain still a second longer. He paced to the window, then back. "Do you have a few minutes now?"

She shut the door behind her. "Assuming my grandmother will arrive shortly, I guess we have a minute or so."

She was all Chandler, polite and formal without being rude. He hated it. "I think I'd feel better if you yelled or screamed or...something."

"Believe me, I've thought about it." Her mouth quirked into the tiniest of smiles.

It only made his heart ache worse. He took a step

toward her, then thought better of it when something very close to pain darted across her face. He'd screwed things up even worse than he thought.

"I wasn't intending to hurt you. I just...I just didn't know what to say."

"Why don't you start with why you couldn't talk to me? Why did you leave without seeing me the other night?"

"Because you belong here. A blind man could see that you're in your element, that you thrive on this. And it's not family obligation. It's in your blood, truly and completely. You said you didn't know what you would feel passionately about in life. Well, I think it's obvious you've found it."

"You're right. I have."

He knew it. And yet the dagger of pain that pierced him in the heart on hearing her say it felt raw and unexpected. "Yeah. Well. What else is there to say, then?"

All pretense of polite decorum fled. "Gee, I don't know. I thought there was a lot left to say. Because I've found a job I enjoy that's not in the neighborhood, that means we have nothing left to say to one another? I guess I thought better of you. I thought you understood."

"I do understand. I understand that our passions are taking us in opposite directions."

"How?" She lifted a hand. "I know I haven't had much time, but neither have you. It doesn't mean I don't want to be with you. I'd spend every spare second with you if I could."

"That's just it, there weren't very many seconds. That's no way to have a relationship."

"I know. I figured that out, too. And if you hadn't left here the other night, I would have told you about the decisions I'd made to help us find a way to make it work."

Nick's pulse raced. "What decisions?"

"Now that the merger is a done deal, I've told my grandfather I'm not ready to take over for him, nor should I at this point. He has very capable people working for him who are in a far better position to run the company than I am."

"But—"

"Let me finish. Do I want to work for him? Absolutely. You're right, I do love it. But I don't love this." She gestured toward the room. "I don't have to choose this just because I choose to work for Chandler Enterprises."

Nick's heart was pounding so loudly in his ears he couldn't absorb all of what she was saying. Hope was building, but he was afraid to allow himself to believe in it again.

"If you'd taken even one of my phone calls, I could have explained all that to you. But no, you take one look at me in a designer gown and decide I'm too good for you. Well, maybe I am, Nick D'Angelo, but it has nothing to do with my address, my bank account or my gene pool."

"Sunny, I—

But she was on a roll and stormed right over him.

"I deserved better, Nick. I deserved to be trusted. I deserved to be involved in decisions that will affect the rest of my life and I resent that you went and decided all on your own what was best for me. For us."

"It wasn't about your gene pool, Sunny," he said softly once she'd finished. There was a fire in her eyes, a passion. Once upon a time that passion had been for him. How had he messed things up so badly? "I honestly thought you did deserve better than me."

"Why?" The fire had left her voice, but not her eyes.

"You belong here. I don't think I do. I just didn't see how we could mix it together and make it work."

"And you wouldn't even let me try?"

"It's been almost four weeks and I can't even see you to try." He lifted his hands. "I know about the merger and why you've been so busy. I didn't even get to tell you how damn proud I am of you."

Her eyes were a little glassy. "You were?"

"I don't resent you loving your life, your work. I want you to be happy. I want you to find the thing that gives you as much satisfaction as running the restaurant gives to me."

"Then why did you leave?"

"Because I wouldn't make you choose. And I believed you'd feel you had to. After a lifetime of being told who you are, you finally found yourself. I didn't think it was right or fair to push. I thought that loving you meant that letting you go was the right thing to do."

"Wait a minute. What did you just say?" She stepped closer.

"I love you, Sunny." He tentatively reached out and brushed a finger down the side of her face. "Your skin is just the finest damn thing I've ever felt," he said, his voice shuddering with emotion. "I want you to be happy. You have spent so much of your life pleasing everyone else. You deserve to have what makes you happy now."

She reached out and pushed his hair off his forehead. "And if what makes me happy is you?"

He was shaking. His entire body. With need, restraint, fear, hope. "Then please, dear God, take it. Take me."

"I love you, too, Nick."

Nothing had ever felt so important, so huge. "I really wanted to talk all this out, and I still do, but I think if I can't take you in my arms right now and kiss you, I'm going to fall apart."

Grinning, Sunny grabbed his arms. It was only when he felt her hands on him that he realized she was trembling as much as he was. "Take me, Nick."

And he did. He thought his need would make the

kiss blindingly ferocious and deep. So it was somewhat startling when he found himself taking her mouth almost reverently, like something to be cherished. And he did cherish her. All of her. She was so special, so real. So his.

And she kissed him the same way. He'd never been made to feel special, cherished. The kiss deepened, tapping into that fierce well of need they both had.

She was so completely tangled in his arms, and he in hers, that they didn't hear the door open. Nor did they hear Vincent clear his throat. The first thing either of them heard was Mama Bennie's loud, "Thank the Lord."

They broke their kiss but not their embrace. In fact, Nick didn't think he'd be letting go of her now or anytime in the near future. His heart swelled with excitement, and his grin was just as huge.

"Mama Bennie, what are you doing here?"

"Visiting my new friend." She turned and motioned behind her. "Franny? Come on in, they're decent."

Frances Chandler entered the room.

Sunny and Nick stood there, wrapped in each other's arms, struck silent in shock.

"Franny?" Nick said.

"Grandmother?" Sunny said.

17

FRANCES SMILED faintly at Bennie, then motioned to the cluster of furniture in the center of the room. "Why don't we all take a seat?"

Nick took Sunny's hand and she clung to it as they all sat, Bennie and Frances in high-backed chairs, Sunny and Nick on the damask-covered couch.

No one spoke. Nick hadn't a clue what to say, and a covert glance at Sunny told him neither did she.

"You might wonder why I called both of you here today," Frances began.

"It was my idea," Bennie added, beaming lovingly at them. She leaned forward and covered their clasped hands. "And I'm so glad I did." Her eyes twinkled as she looked at Frances. She covered her hand, as well. "I knew if I just spoke to your grandmother, we'd find a way to make this all work out."

"Why did you think you needed to do anything?" she said to her grandmother. "I never even mentioned Nick to you."

"I'm aware of that." Frances said it with no hint of anything other than a polite commentary, but there was no doubt of her hurt.

Abashed, Sunny, said, "I knew you had enough to deal with and I just didn't think—"

"You didn't think I'd approve."

Sunny's cheeks went pink. "I...well..."

Frances's expression softened slightly, and her shoulders rounded. "Susan, I'm aware that I've never encouraged confidences of yours. But I had hoped you'd have enough of a conviction in the man you loved to tell us when the time came."

Sunny sat up straighter, bristling. "I'm not ashamed of Nick. Why would I have hired him to handle the gala if I didn't think the world of him?"

"I'm not talking about his business acumen. I'm quite well aware of his abilities in that regard. We have a waiting list of people eager to reserve him for their upcoming functions."

"Wait a minute." Nick broke in. "I am in the room, here." But no one was listening.

"You do?" Sunny said to Frances.

Nick turned to her. "Is that so unbelievable?"

"Of course not." She threw her arms around him and hugged him. "That's wonderful!"

"Now, see?" Bennie said. She turned to Frances. "I told you this would all work out." She patted Frances's knee. "Now go ahead, tell them the rest of it."

Sunny still held Nick's hand, but her attention was riveted on her grandmother. "The rest of what?" Her heart was so full of love and hope, and yet suddenly she was filled with apprehension. "Is it about Grand-father?"

"In a way," Frances said. When she saw the fear in her granddaughter's expression, she quickly added, "He's resting comfortably upstairs. He's not in any danger."

Sunny pressed her hand to her chest. "Oh, thank goodness." Nick squeezed her hand, and she smiled at him. It reminded her of other things she still had to do. And no time would be better than now. "Grand-mother, I have to talk to you. I want my own life in addition to working for Chandler Enterprises. I've al-ready spoken to Grandfather and he's giving me a hard time. So I spoke to Cambridge and set the wheels into motion anyway. I'm firm about this deci-sion—"

"My dear, please. I know. Cambridge still reports to your grandfather. We're well aware of your deci-sion to scale back your duties at Chandler Enter-prises."

"You are? And Grandfather, what did he say?"

Bennie broke in again. "We can discuss business later. You're not putting it off again, Franny."

That was the second time she'd called her that. And her grandmother didn't even flinch! "How did you two say you met again?"

"I ran into Franny that day I was here talking with you about the catering. She was coming in as I was getting ready to leave after speaking to Mary Anne."

She smiled fondly at Frances, who looked only marginally uncomfortable with the sudden focus. That she allowed even that much to show was remarkable. "We had a nice chat about the both of you."

"You did?" This from Nick and Sunny.

"Yes," Frances said. "We did. Bennie and I have found we share some common ground. And after talking, we both agreed that you two should be together."

"You did?" Again, they spoke at the same time.

Frances frowned at their outburst, but Sunny's grin would not be restrained.

"Franny understands all about choosing family honor over love."

Sunny's smile faltered. She looked at her grandmother, and for the first time thought about what she might have been like as a young woman, filled with the same hopes and dreams Sunny had. "I always thought you'd chosen Grandfather and life as a Chandler because you wanted it."

"My family did a great deal for me, but they also expected a great deal of me. Marrying Edwin was in everyone's best interests."

"You mean...you didn't love him?" Why this shocked her she had no idea. They'd certainly never been anyone's idea of a love match, not in the overt sense, anyway. "But you've done everything for him."

"I did it for both of us. I believe it's fair to say the

rewards we've reaped have far exceeded our expectations. Don't misunderstand me, Susan. I have a great deal of respect for your grandfather, as he does for me."

"But..." Her mouth dropped open as comprehension dawned. "There was someone else, wasn't there?" She knew she was right. Frances was unable to hide the flash of pain. "That had to have been over fifty years ago."

"If you and Nick were forced to be apart, do you think you'd forget him? Or how he makes you feel?" This was from Bennie. Frances nodded her agreement.

It was the closest thing Sunny had ever had to a personal conversation with her grandmother, and she couldn't believe she was having it here, with Nick and his grandmother listening! "No. I would have gone on with my life. But I would never forgive myself for choosing family obligations over personal happiness."

"Nor should you." Her grandmother looked away, seemingly needing a moment to collect herself.

Bennie stepped in. "This is our common ground, Niccolo."

Now it was Nick's turn to gape. "Now wait a minute. I know for a fact you and Sal were very much in love."

Bennie's face lit up. "Yes, yes we were. I was expected to stay home after my mother died and help my father raise my younger brothers. I was the oldest, it was my place."

"But you didn't," Sunny said in a hushed tone.

"No. I met Salvatore and made a very difficult decision to leave Italy with him and come to America. I was only seventeen. I worried many times about my father and my brothers, but I never regretted giving myself happiness. I went back to Italy after we started the restaurant and spoke to my father. He was filled with bitterness and never forgave me. But my brothers, both happily married, understood my decision."

"Bennie didn't want—" After a glance from Mama Bennie, she corrected herself. "*We* didn't want you to feel you had to choose, like we did. Between family and love."

Sunny left her seat, knelt in front of her grandmother and embraced her. It was awkward, and Frances was still obviously coming to terms with everything, but she embraced her back. It was more than Sunny could have ever hoped for. A beginning. Her eyes were shining with tears when she sat next to Nick again. "Thank you." She sniffed, then laughed. "This is the best gift you've ever given me."

When Frances looked confused, Sunny clarified. "Your love."

Frances's eyes instantly were wet with tears, shocking both her and Sunny. "Oh, darling, you've always had our love. I know we're not entirely comfortable with public displays, but I never realized—" She stopped, took Bennie's offer of a lace-trimmed hankie and dabbed her eyes.

"It's okay, Grandmother. It's okay." And it was. Sunny treasured this breakthrough with her grandmother, but she was realistic enough to know that some things wouldn't change. She doubted she'd ever have the close relationship with Frances that Nick had with Bennie, but this was already so much more than she thought she'd ever have. "Does Grandfather know? About all this?" Her eyes widened. "Does he know about...that you married him and loved someone else?"

Frances nodded. "We might not be the love match of the century, Susan, be we are very well suited to one another. Your grandfather is my closest and dearest friend. And that is more than I ever thought I'd have."

"As you are mine."

Everyone jumped and turned to find Edwin standing in the doorway, clad in a dressing gown and resting heavily on a cane.

"Oh, dear, you shouldn't be up so soon." Frances stood and went toward him.

"Now, now, Frances. I can determine where I want to be in my own home and if I'm fit enough to be there."

No one said anything.

"You are my closest friend, Frances. And my biggest champion. You are aware that there is no one else who has as much of my love and respect as you do."

All three women in the room had tears in their eyes. Nick made a suspicious swipe at his.

"Edwin, please," Frances bade him, looking almost desperate at this highly unusual display. "This can wait."

He walked slowly into the room. "No, it can't. In fact, I have done a lot of thinking these past weeks, and realize that time isn't that forgiving to those who wait for the right moment." He turned to his granddaughter. "Susan, I owe you an apology. I have always known you belonged at Chandler and perhaps I was impatient with your obstinacy."

"Grandfather—"

He tilted his cane toward her, signaling she was to let him continue. She did.

"I was impatient because I knew my health was failing me and I needed you there for me. Your decision to go *find yourself* couldn't have come at a worse time."

"If you had just told me—"

"No. And I'm glad now that I didn't. We both needed to go find ourselves."

"But you were right, I do love working for Chandler Enterprises."

"But you also need more than that. You need a full life. And I believe this young man and his delightful grandmother are a part of that life." He turned to a blushing Bennie and nodded. "Thank you for talking with my wife and me so frankly. Your wisdom has proven an excellent source of guidance to us both. I hope you will continue to set us straight when the need arises."

Bennie laughed, her eyes still shiny with unshed tears. "I would consider it an honor, Eddie."

To his credit, his wince was barely visible. Sunny swallowed a laugh, then sat ramrod straight when her grandfather said, "Now, Nick. Can I call you Nick?"

Nick stood and took Edwin's outstretched hand. "Please, sir."

"Are you aware of what you're getting into here?"

Nick grinned. "I don't think so, sir. But I've never been one to turn my back on a challenge."

"Well, Susan will definitely be that and more."

"Grandfather!"

Nick was chuckling. "Actually, sir, I was thinking more in terms of you and your lovely wife."

Edwin smiled. "Good, good. Just so you understand."

"Oh, I understand. We're well aware we'll have a whole lot of people looking over our shoulders, making sure we take good care of one another."

Sunny stood and slipped her hand in Nick's. "And we wouldn't have it any other way."

"Good, good," Edwin said again. He lifted his cane and rapped Nick lightly on the shin. "Well, boy, don't just stand there, sweep her off her feet. She needs more of that in her life, and we're just not equipped to give it to her." He turned and motioned to Frances. "Ring Vincent and have him serve our best champagne."

Nick realized Edwin was giving him an opening to discreetly leave with Sunny, and he wasn't about to pass it up. He took her into his arms and kissed her. When he lifted his head, he purposely avoiding looking at the other three occupants of the room. He was certain Bennie was beaming in approval, but he knew his future in-laws would take some time to adjust to such...public displays of emotion. He was prepared to give them many opportunities, and soon.

He tucked her hand in his, and they'd almost made their getaway when he stopped short. "Wait. I forgot something. Something really important."

"What?" Edwin, Frances and Bennie all spoke at once.

Nick and Sunny turned to find the older three staring at them. So much for sneaking away.

Keeping Sunny's hand in his, he crossed the room to Edwin and extended his other hand. "I'd like to formally ask for your granddaughter's hand in marriage."

Edwin nodded in approval and shook Nick's hand. "Granted." Then he grinned. "Just remember, no returns."

"Not on your life. I plan to do this right." Nick turned and got down on one knee.

"Nick, you don't have to— Please, get up." Sunny looked at her grandparents and Bennie, then at him. "This really isn't—" What was she doing? This was the most romantic, wonderful moment in her life.

"Will you marry me, Sunny Chandler?"

She laughed even as tears of joy sprang to her eyes. She helped Nick to his feet and kissed him soundly on the mouth. "Yes. Yes, yes, yes." She grinned. "Now, can we go back to that feet-sweeping thing my grandfather mentioned? I rather liked that."

"So did I." Bennie shrugged when everyone looked at her in surprise. "I'm a sentimental old fool."

Nick swung a laughing Sunny into his arms and headed for the door.

"You realize they'll be down here naming our children before we even set the wedding date," Nick whispered in her ear as the door shut behind them. Then he groaned.

"What?"

"I just realized she'll be telling my sisters."

"Oh, let her have her fun." She nipped at his earlobe, making him groan again. "After all, it's only fair since we'll be having ours."

Nick stopped at the base of the sweeping staircase. "I don't think I can wait until we get home. Which room is yours?"

Sunny laughed and motioned upward.

Nick kicked the door open to her room. Suite of rooms, he amended.

She must have seen the look on his face, because she nuzzled his ear and said, "I was sort of hoping I could move in with you if that's okay. Unless, of course, you had your heart set on moving in here."

Nick wandered through the room and finally found the right door to her bedroom. He tried to be tactful. "I, um, wasn't planning on it." Then he saw the ocean of down mattress and the sea of pillows she called a bed. He smiled as he fell onto it, cradling her against him. "But we could compromise and move your bed to my place."

"Our place."

He rolled over so she was half beneath him. Looking down into her lovely face, he couldn't believe she was really his. "Our place. Our life."

"Our two families," she added wryly. "It probably won't be easy."

"Nothing worth having ever is." He leaned down and kissed her. "I love you, Sunny." Wonder filled him. "How is it you went looking for yourself and ended up finding me?"

"Maybe I found myself in you. I think I realized that you never stop discovering who you are."

"So you won't mind me shaking things up once in a while?"

She shook her head. "I was sort of counting on it.

There's no law against having a lifelong fling with your husband, is there?"

"Not that I know of. What say we start shaking things up right now? Wanna walk on the wild side with me right here in Haddon Hall?" He rolled to his back and pulled her astride him. Her skirt hiked up high enough on her thighs to reveal thin lace garter straps.

"When—" The word came out a dry croak. "When did you start wearing those?" he asked weakly.

Her expression could only be described as smug. She slowly unhooked first one side, then the other. "Maybe you'll be discovering a few new things about me, as well." She shimmied her skirt up. Her panties were held together with the merest wisp of lace. She grabbed one side and yanked. "Come on. Let's get wild."

_____Epilogue_____

THE SUN was setting and the air was finally cooling off. Twinkling lights flickered on, illuminating the surrounding trees. The buffet tables were thinning out as everyone drifted to the dance floor to watch the bride and groom take their first turn as husband and wife.

Andrea sniffed as she held her husband's hand. "They are even more gorgeous together than I thought they'd be." Callie was holding her other hand. Her little bridesmaid dress was adorable, with matching sprigs of flowers woven in her curls. You hardly even noticed the sauce stains on her chin...or the matching ones on the front of her dress.

B.J. rubbed her taut tummy and smiled as she felt her husband's hand kneading the ache in her back. Maybe she'd take a turn around the dance floor, after all. Suddenly she was feeling a bit lighter.

Marina scolded her kids for the hundredth time, then turned to clap when Nick executed a smooth dip to the laughing delight of his new wife. So she finally had a sister-in-law. Boy, was this going to be fun.

Rachel leaned in between her sisters. "So, when do

we take bets on the first baby, huh?" They all laughed, then drifted onto the dance floor with their husbands, children tumbling after them.

Bennie settled back in her chair, wishing Sal could be here to see his oldest grandson so vibrantly and happily married. She tapped her foot along with the orchestra. They weren't so bad. It hadn't been her idea, but since Franny had relented to having the wedding outdoors *and* catered by D'Angelos, giving in on the music seemed a small thing. She sighed, thinking back over the service. It couldn't have been more lovely. Father Sartori had beamed throughout the sermon and had even wiped his eyes when Nick and Sunny had spoken their personally written vows at the end.

She looked at Edwin. He'd given a wonderful if slightly stuffy toast. Still, she didn't miss the look of admiration in his eyes as Sunny twirled by. Bennie smiled. She'd have plenty of time to work on him. He'd loosen up yet.

She helped herself to two glasses of champagne as a waiter passed by, then turned to Frances and handed her one. "Well, I think it's all gone quite well, don't you?" Bennie tried to hide her smile as yet another D'Angelo youngster went flying past, feet pounding, with two more little ones right on her heels. Franny did look a mite…overwhelmed. But she had plenty of stamina and good breeding. Bennie had faith she'd adapt. Eventually.

"Yes, I believe it did," Frances finally said. Her calm was belied by the larger than acceptable swallow she took. Her fourth glass.

Yes, everything had turned out well indeed. Bennie lifted her glass in a silent toast heavenward. *Well, Sal, five of them are happily taken care of and giving us great-grandbabies. Or will be shortly, if I know anything about anything.*

Joey popped up at that moment and kissed his grandmother soundly on the cheek. "Any chance my best girl will give me a dance?"

Bennie flushed with pleasure but shooed him on. "Surely there are other young ladies out there who can keep up with you better than I can. Go on now." She turned to Frances and patted her on the knee. "Handsome boy, isn't he? And bright, too. Did I tell you he already has job offers in the computer technology field?"

One of the older D'Angelos raced by, snatching a sloshing glass of champagne from the sticky fingers of her little one. She smiled frantically, then handed the glass to a startled Frances before taking off after the chubby toddler.

Bennie laughed, but was not to be deterred. "So, I understand Chandler's new CEO has a granddaughter about Joey's age, am I right?"

Frances Chandler nodded and smiled faintly...then downed the contents of the sticky glass of champagne in one gulp.

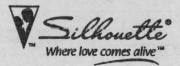

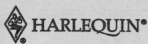

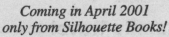

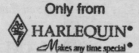

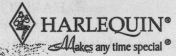